Murder takes a Bow

CHARMAIN Z. BRACKETT

Published November 2019

This book is dedicated to my best friend Pam Henry who died Aug. 14, 2019. Pam was diagnosed with ovarian cancer in August 2017. She shouldn't have lived those last two years, but she overcame the disease for a while. I'm grateful for your extended time.

Thank you, Pam, for reading my books and for encouraging me. Thanks for our many adventures. I'll figure out a way to write about them and finish some of the things we weren't able to do together on this side. I'll wear my teal ribbon and keep our memories close. I love you, Pam. Until we meet again, my friend - bubbles, butterflies, happy dolphins, London.

To my readers - My hope is that those of you who've read the Grace series to this point would consider making a trip to Augusta, Georgia, Grace's hometown and mine. I hope I've painted a picture of a town you'd like to visit. In some of my books, I've disguised the names. In other places, I've used real ones, but if you come and look hard enough, you can find the places mentioned. It's more beautiful than I describe it, and there's plenty to do. Check us out on the web and plan a visit. Just don't try to come here the first full week of April unless you already have a way to get to the tournament. Trust me on that one.

1

I'd seen plenty of crime shows. There was always one episode with a macho rookie cop called to his first murder investigation. He's usually shown rushing away from it with his hand over his mouth. Then you see him bent over and throwing up everything he'd eaten in the past several hours. Despite having a weak stomach and finding three dead bodies, I'd never thrown up before. There's a first time for everything, I suppose.

Maybe my brain didn't take in all the previous scenes. With two of the bodies, there wasn't really any blood; with Bill Andrews' death, I was focused on his widow, not the scene. This time, however, I was alone. And this scene was much different from the rest.

I won't go into all the gory details. And it was definitely gory. It was violent, and I knew it was personal.

Murder wasn't pretty. It wasn't funny. I'd thought it might get easier with each body I found, but it never did.

As I stood in the middle of a stage with a spotlight focused on the lifeless body of a man with whom I'd exchanged words only a few hours before, I tried not to look at the body, but at the same time, I couldn't help myself. I tried to soak in every detail. There was no doubt this was a murder – not an accident and not a suicide. I wasn't an expert, but he had a gaping wound in the back of his head. He couldn't have done that himself. Besides, if he'd fallen in such a way to injure the back of his head, wouldn't he be lying face up instead of face down in a pool of his own blood? And oh, the blood! Did I mention that already? So much of it! Maybe it was a good thing I couldn't see his face. There were too many other faces forever seared into my mind. As gruesome as it was, I tried not to stare; I tried to look away. But I couldn't help myself.

I noticed his cell phone smashed next to him. Did he have time to think about making a call? Did he know the danger that was near him? Did he want to call a loved one? Did he have anyone who would miss him?

Shock was so familiar to me. I think I had muscle memory of what to do next. Standing there over the corpse, I went through the same array of emotions I always did. Except that this time, I felt sick. My stomach lurched, and I ran backstage and found a trash can. I threw up everything I'd eaten earlier. I walked back toward the stage and slid to the floor near the wing. My first thought went to Drew. He was the expert; he knew what to do. Besides, even if I simply called 911, Drew would be on the scene. That's what he did as a homicide investigator, and I needed one of those.

The only thing was I hadn't spoken to Drew in three months. And the last time I saw him, he was standing in the middle of our house, and I was throwing myself at him begging him not to leave me. Not that it worked because he left anyway; we were still no longer married. I mulled these thoughts over in my head as I stared at the body. I couldn't even scream.

I pulled my cell phone out of my purse. I never took his number out of my contacts, not that I'd forget it. I never had a reason to call him anymore. When our house sold, Trevor advised me to send a lawyer to conduct the transaction on my behalf. That way I didn't have to see Drew. I agreed it was a good idea. I didn't feel like having the wounds re-opened. They'd slowly started to heal, I think. Sometimes I wasn't sure. Sometimes, I still cried myself to sleep wondering what I could've done differently to make him stay. My stomach sank even lower. I felt sick again.

But I had to do something. I couldn't just walk out of the

theater and leave a dead body center-stage, or could I? It was tempting – to walk, no run and hide. Let someone else figure it all out for a change. I swallowed hard and took a deep breath before making the call. The phone rang a couple of times before he answered.

"Grace?"

My name was a question. I'm sure he couldn't imagine why I was calling. I couldn't speak at first. Different body, different crime scene, same response with me. I was never able to think too clearly when I stumbled upon a murder.

"Hi, Drew, I'm sorry," I paused. I was aware that my voice was cracking. I couldn't finish the sentence, but it was okay. Drew had picked up on it. We'd been through this before. He knew me.

"Grace, what's wrong? Are you okay?" he asked.

Words seemed to fail me.

"No," I whispered.

"Where are you?"

"In the auditorium at Augusta Tech."

"I'm on my way."

The morning had started like any other. I'd gotten to the shop early. It was a quiet Monday. No one would be in until around 11 o'clock.

I bought a smoothie for breakfast and sipped on it through a paper straw. It was called the Green Dragon smoothie from the Half Moon Cantina. It was a delicious mix of yogurt, peanut butter, kale, banana and some other things thrown in. It was bright green. My mother always told me to eat green food. Greens made you strong, and there was kale in it. That should've counted for something, right?

I enjoyed the quiet March morning alone and began doodling in a notebook I'd bought. I'd been experimenting with colored pencils and charcoal. I was no artist, but it was fun to dabble in what came so easily to Emmie. It was a slow Monday, and I drew the morning away until a voice broke into my reverie.

"Is that a sketchbook you have there, Grace?"

I glanced up to see a curious Emmie. I quickly snapped my

notebook closed, away from her prying eyes.

She narrowed her gazed at me.

"It's nothing, Emmie."

She held out her hand.

"Come on, sweetie, it's me you're talking to. I've never known you to draw."

I stood up from my desk and pulled the notebook close to my chest.

"You're the artist here, not me."

Emmie put her hands on her hips.

"Grace, you have always had a good eye. What are you hiding from me?"

I took a breath.

"I read somewhere that art is therapeutic, or maybe it was you who told me that, Emmie. I can't remember now."

"First of all, art isn't good therapy. No, it's great therapy. Now that my FBI stint is over, I find myself drawing more and more. Of course, it helps that I have an art exhibition coming up at the end of next month or have you forgotten? Slinging paint on canvas is great too. You should join me some time." she said and smiled. "It's definitely better for the hips than our 'death by chocolate' girls' nights."

I laughed.

"No, I haven't forgotten about your show. You're having it here. And my hips don't miss our girls' nights in front of your TV. But I do."

She gave me a quick hug.

"Besides, Emmie, you have nothing to worry about. I'm not very good – at drawing, that is. I won't be competing with you for an art show," I said as I opened one page. Some of my pencil drawings were of flower arrangements she'd done. Others were attempts at faces, the faces of the people who I'd seen die in the past year. I even tried to sketch Bill Andrews who was one of my least favorites. I didn't want her to see those though. Drawing seemed to help. She folded her arms across her chest and grinned at me.

"I'm glad to know I'm rubbing off on you, sweetie," she said. "Maybe it's time for an Emmie and Grace art exhibition, but after my solo show."

She winked at me as I vigorously shook my head "no."

"I just said that I wouldn't compete with you for an exhibition."

"I never said anything about a competition. I said a joint exhibition."

"No, Emmie, these are things I don't want anyone else to see."

She smiled at me. I knew she understood what I was saying.

"Anything else in there?" she asked as she looked at the one drawing I'd allowed her to see.

I'd also been doodling some of my ideas for an upcoming project. I didn't always do that. Usually, I just presented my portfolio when someone was interested in designs. They'd light onto something similar, and we'd tweak it from there. I'm not sure why I'd picked up a sketch pad. I suppose I needed some other creative outlet. I'd always admired Emmie for her artistic abilities. I'd wanted to be like her. Flowers helped me get rid of some of the negative emotions I'd still been working through over the past couple of months, but I needed more help than flowers could give on their own. I wasn't sure art was it though. I didn't think my sketches were all that great, and that gave the perfectionist side of me more stress. It was a catch-22.

"You, Beth, and I share a lot of similar traits and habits. Besides, I've always been jealous of your artistic abilities. You know that," I said as I pulled the sketchpad back and debated on whether to show her anything else.

"They're pretty good, Grace," she said.

"Thanks."

"No, I mean it. I could show you some techniques on our next girls' night."

I forced a smile.

"That would be nice."

"So what else is in there?"

"Just a few potential ideas for our next big job."

"For that English lady?"

"You mean Gemma?"

"Yes, her," Emmie said and wrinkled her nose.

"You don't like Gemma?"

"I don't really know her, but you sure do spend a lot of time with her."

"Emmie, you're being ridiculous."

"Grace, you, Emmie, and I are like the Three Musketeers. We don't want to be broken up," Beth interjected.

"She's just a customer."

"That's what you said about Trevor," she said as she put her hands on her hips and cocked her head to one side.

I folded my arms against my chest

"Well, Trevor was a customer. And he didn't break up any relationships – zero. It's also true about Gemma. She seems really nice and a bit lonely."

Emmie reached out and gave me a quick hug.

"You know I'm just teasing you about Trevor. I wasn't trying to imply Trevor broke you and Drew up. I know Trevor didn't break up your marriage. But this Gemma person acts like she's your new best friend. And speaking of Trevor. Since he came along, our girls' nights have gotten even more scarce. We need one and soon. Can you break away from the handsome doc for a night?"

"You mean you need our 'gorge on sugar and induce a chocolate coma after crying into a box of tissue' night?"

Emmie folded her arms against her chest.

"Gee, when you put it like that, it doesn't sound nearly as fun, Grace, but yes, that's exactly what I mean."

I laughed.

"It's not funny, Grace. I miss the times you and I spent together." I miss you."

"I miss you too, Emmie."

"Well, the next time the two of you decide to do that, you'd better invite me. I haven't been invited to one in forever, and I'm hurt," Beth said as she pretended to pout.

I put my hands on my hips and shook my head.

"Like I said, Emmie, you're being ridiculous. I admit that I have seen Gemma a lot, but I'm not as trusting of new people as I was at one time. Since a few have tried to kill me, I have my guard up. Not that I expect Gemma to try to kill me, but you never know. I'm leaving it open to the possibility," I said sarcastically and smiled at Emmie. She simply glared in return. "And Beth, I promise the next time we OD on chocolate, you'll be invited. You'd better bring extra."

"Deal," Beth said.

I gave a weak laugh, Emmie ignored me. I wasn't sure why all the jealousy over Gemma, who was an English instructor at Augusta Tech. She'd come into the picture about a month before, and I'd been at her office several times to discuss what she had in mind.

"Why are you looking at me like that, Emmie?"

"Because I think she's up to something."

"Why? I mean she's got big plans for her job. It's exciting. I enjoy hearing about it. They haven't really had a theater department at the school even though there's a great space on campus. She's bringing one to life there. She's written a few plays, and they are having this huge theater festival in the fall. This first play is to test the waters so to speak. She's also working on some movie ideas too and a program for that as well."

"At a technical college?" Emmie asked skeptically.

"You can't put on a show without technical people. There's lights and sound and sets that have to be built. If you have anything special like flying, there's all sorts of technical stuff involved. Putting on a show is more than just actors in costume. You should know that. And don't forget about hair and makeup – that could involve the cosmetology department."

"So, what's our part in all of this?"

"I thought I'd shared this with you already. There's a gala to raise money for the program. They want to start a new movie and theater technical branch with all the entertainment that is coming out of Atlanta these days. There's a hope that some of this will shift into Augusta."

"Yeah, that's true, Grace. There was that movie, The Mule, about the oldest-ever courier for a Mexican drug cartel that was filmed here. I know a lot of local people who were extras in it. There have been international companies, and Augusta has a huge indie filmmaking community. I read about it in the paper not long ago. And I've heard about a couple of film festivals here, but I've never gone. I think you usually have us busy with a wedding or something."

She winked at me.

"Gemma needs your expertise anyway, Emmie. You're the one who makes all the gorgeous flower arrangements, not me."

"I've always said you were way too hard on yourself, Grace, but thanks for the compliment."

"Is that all you're doing?" Beth asked. She tilted her head to the side. I knew what she was thinking. I'd told her the rest.

I smiled proudly.

"What – besides the fact that she's asked me to be in her play?"

"Really?" Emmie asked.

I guess I hadn't told her. I was still distracted these days. I knew it, but I tried to act like I wasn't. I'm sure they all saw through me.

"Yes. I told her about the shows I did in high school. She wrote in a part for me. I even have two lines," I said excitedly. "It's something different. My little part is of a florist

Emmie folded her arms.

"What?" I asked.

"You. You're acting crazy, and you don't act like someone who is distrustful."

"After what we've been through in the past year, I don't trust people like I used to. And there's something about all of this that I can't put my finger on, Emmie, but I'm having fun. I have my first rehearsal tomorrow night."

With her arms still folded across her chest, Emmie tapped her fingers on her upper arms and raised her eyebrow at me.

"Grace, I can't figure you out."

"Fine. Just help me out with these plans. I'm supposed to meet her this afternoon. We're going to need a couple of Emmie designs for this. You know, the over-the-top ones you're so good at."

"You know what they say about flattery, Grace."

"That it will get me everywhere with you," I said and laughed. Beth laughed too.

"She's got you on that one. Compliments go a long way with you, Emmie, and you know it," Beth interjected.

"Fine, but if you have a new bestie, you have to include us," Emmie grumbled.

"I don't know much about Gemma except that she's actually from England. She married an American in London, and they moved here. But I'm not sure about their relationship. I think they're separated or it's complicated or something. Anyway, she loves theater and English literature and is teaching here. She's trying to get into a doctoral program and doesn't plan on staying where she is. She'd like to establish something, make it successful, and move on to a four-year college. This gala is a big deal for her."

"When is the gala?"

"Three weeks. I have to meet with her today to talk about the flowers she's going to need for the show. We're down to the wire."

"Four weeks, so right after the tournament?

"Yes, a week after the tournament. That makes it difficult with people being gone."

"We have the gala. Then, we have a play," Emmie said.

"Basically, yes. I've got all the details written down. I know I can count on you to make this amazing."

"Grace, you know you can count on me - and Beth."

"Thanks."

"The whole thing sounds fun, and I'm just giving you a hard time. I don't see you outside of work as much as I used to, and I know it has to do with a handsome, blond doctor," Emmie said and winked at me.

"Trevor is," I started the sentence, but Emmie and Beth finished it with me. "just a friend."

Emmie grinned at me.

"Friends don't make you smile the way I see you smile when you think no one is looking at you."

I put my hands on my hips and shook my head at her.

"Stop barking up this tree, Emmie and Beth."

"Well, he has been good for you," Beth interjected.

"I'll agree. He has been good for me. He's been a great friend, and so have the two of you. Now, on that note, I have some work to do so I can keep the two of you employed."

I packed up my sketchpad and portfolio and headed to my car. It wasn't a long drive, but it was enough time for me to clear my head. Trevor kept me sane and was there for me without prying. Emmie and Beth were experts at prying. Since I knew their M.O., I could skirt around things with them. I told people only what they needed to know, and I didn't argue with most people's assumptions. I kept a lot of things to myself, but I was sure my closest two friends didn't believe my façade. I liked that Gemma didn't ask me about my love life. I was just Grace, the floral designer. She only had expectations of my flowers. I didn't have to hide anything either, like I did with everyone else.

What I didn't tell anyone, not even Trevor, was that I had nightmares. As if my dreams weren't bad enough, now I spent many nights afraid. I woke up in a cold sweat, feeling the pressure of a phantom gun barrel buried in my temple. I kept my own gun close to me. I was afraid to put it under my pillow, but it was close enough for me to reach it. I hoped it was anyway. Even though I was living above my brother's garage, and Zack could be there in a split second, I couldn't shake the things I'd seen and experienced over the past year.

As always, flowers were a saving grace so to speak. They kept me sane. Faith seemed far away at times, but Trevor had become a rock for me to lean on. His own quiet faith helped me more than he could've known. He cared for me like no one ever had; not counting my mother, of course. He was kind, considerate, and so patient.

Nevertheless, I still found myself thinking of Drew at times and being upset with myself that I couldn't save our marriage. It had only been three months since our divorce was finalized, five months since Drew walked out on me. Trevor had become my best friend, but I was torn between losing him and letting him completely into my heart. He wanted me to see a therapist, but I kept putting it off. I never stayed the night at his house because I didn't want him to know certain things. Like the fact that I didn't sleep. That I had nightmares. And that I slept with a gun. It was stupid to think he didn't know at least some of it. He could tell something was wrong. He knew I wasn't completely honest with him when he asked how I was. I could see it by the look in his eyes. Besides, I never was good at lying. He knew better than to believe my protests about my being fine.

I tried to fill my mind with other things, so I didn't think of dead bodies and dead marriages. I'd started sketching; I'd tried to read more; I'd even thrown a few words into a journal. With Drew's earlier investigations, I'd started researching things again. I had a business degree, but I minored in English in college. I liked doing research papers and finding facts. I even liked creative writing, and the act of research somehow had stimulated my love of words. Some people might've called those words in my journal poetry. I wasn't sure I'd call them that. It didn't matter because they were for my eyes only. When I couldn't sleep, I'd get up and either get on my computer to research, read a book, or scribble my random thoughts into my journal.

Gemma was a relative newcomer to the area and asked me tons of questions about Augusta. Some of the reading I'd been doing was brushing up on my Augusta history to help her. She seemed fascinated by it and the famous people who'd once called the town home. I rolled over some facts in my brain just in case I needed to retrieve them.

Augusta Tech is in south Augusta. Some of the southernmost parts of the county are still rural, complete with farms and a couple of dairies dotting the landscape. The area became more suburban in the 1950s with the construction of what many in my mother's generation and older call "the bomb plant." The Savannah River Site was constructed in the Aiken area across the Savannah River in South Carolina then. It brought an influx of workers, and more homes filled Augusta's southside. More growth was fueled in the 1960s with Fort Gordon, an Army installation. The government sector with the military and SRS, the medical community and academia are key components in Augusta's economy.

I didn't remember how I got to the college. My grandmother had lived in south Augusta when I was younger, so we drove out there a lot. When I learned to drive, my mother taught me the back roads, so I knew all kinds of alternate routes to get where I was headed. Lately much of my driving around town had been muscle memory. That probably wasn't a good thing to admit. I was so distracted, but I tried to drive extra slowly to compensate.

I sat in the parking lot for a few moments before going in. I had to pull myself together and talk myself into my role of business professional. I took a quick breath and headed inside.

I thought about clever things to say. Gemma probably knew about Augusta's academic side. I graduated from what was once known as Augusta State University. Before that, it was Augusta College – a four-year liberal arts college in the heart of Summerville. We're also home to the Southeast's third oldest medical college. The Medical College of Georgia was founded in 1828. A few years ago, the state decided to merge Augusta State with the Medical College of Georgia. There was much hoopla about the name. The president of the combined universities disregarded a community survey and dubbed it Georgia Regents University. I knew few Augustans who could say that name without uttering disdain for the college president. To the joy of many, he finally left, and the college got the name everyone except that former president wanted - Augusta University. The most recent addition to Augusta University is a cyber college which ties back into Fort Gordon and its mission to train soldiers in cyber security. We also have the technical college where Gemma works as well as an historically black college named Paine College, where author Frank Yerby graduated from. Yerby was a famous novelist. In the 1940s and 1950s, he broke through racial barriers. His books, Foxes of Harrow and The Saracen Blade, were transformed into films.

With my factoids in place, I walked into the building and found Gemma in her office down a long cinderblock-walled corridor. She used her hands when she talked. The more excited she was about a subject, the more her hands moved. She was in the mid-30s with long brown hair and a sweet smile. She was one of those people who never met a stranger. Within five minutes of meeting her, she acted as though you were her new best friend. Emmie was right on that account although I had tried to keep her at a distance, which was no small feat.

"This is going to be the best show ever. I just know it," she said to the woman in the office with her.

I knocked on the door because she was in a lively conversation with her hands flailing about

"Oh, Grace, it's so good to see you," she said and gave me a hug. "This is Carolyn. She's the department's administrative assistant. She just joined us at the beginning of the school year, but she's awesome. She keeps us all on schedule."

She let go as she pulled me into the room with them.

"And this is Grace. She will make this play and party dazzle. I knew it from the minute I walked into her shop and met her and Emmie."

I shook Carolyn's hand.

"It's nice to meet you," I said.

"I've heard so many things about you," she replied.

"Good things I hope."

"I could never say anything bad about you, Grace," Gemma said. "Oh Grace, we were talking about flowers and looking online."

"What do you think about camellias?" interjected Carolyn, who was in her mid-50s and slightly overweight. She had a silver bobbed haircut.

I smiled.

"Camellias are among my favorites. The South loves them too; they grow well here during the winter. My mother has the most beautiful camellias. There are so many varieties of them."

Gemma beamed.

"I need some," Gemma said. "I love them too."

"Well, I'm not sure that would work. They have a long growing season around here, but by the gala they will be hard to find. They are a kiss from Heaven during the dismal winter days of December and January. The ones in my mother's yard bloom around Christmas, and she has others that bloom in February. They tend to stop blooming in March or April.

Carolyn's face fell.

"I simply love camellias," Gemma said excitedly. She seemed not to notice Carolyn. "Do you think you could find some, love? They are integral to the play. Our main character is named Camellia."

"I'll see what I can do, but you may have to settle for silk."

"Silk would be fine as long as they look like the real thing. I like this one," she said pointing to her computer screen.

I moved closer and leaned in.

"Did you know that there are more than 2,000 types of camellias? So, finding a specific one could be difficult. Camellias are grown in many parts of the world and are said to have originated in China, where they are the symbol of luck for the New Year. We have tons of varieties of camellias in Augusta. There are a couple of camellia groups and a big camellia show every year – usually in January."

"You seem to know a lot about camellias," said Carolyn.

"I do. I propagated some from my mother's and put them

in my," I paused midsentence. I used to have camellias, azaleas and all types of flowers in my yard, but for a minute, I forgot I didn't have a yard. I missed my own flowers. I swallowed and thought of something to fill in the dead space. I tried to fake a smile. "Flowers are my business. I should know a thing or two about them. But as I said, they are coming to the end of their blooming season."

"Well, Grace, I trust you to make it work," said Gemma.

"I love camellias. They remind me of where I grew up; lots of camellias there too," said Carolyn, as she turned her head away. She seemed upset. I wondered where she was from. I couldn't place her accent although the way she said a couple of things reminded me of someone. I just wasn't sure who. Gemma kept talking. I wanted to touch Carolyn's arm to comfort her, but I didn't. I just stood there as Gemma chatted excitedly. I had no idea what she was saying.

"Don't you think so, Grace?" was the next thing I heard Gemma say. I had zoned out, and she was staring straight at me.

"I'm sorry. What did you say?"

"Don't you think it would be a good idea for you to work with some of the horticulture students here? We can bring in a lot of different departments. They don't have floral design here. Maybe you can teach some of the students the art of flower arranging," she said with a hopeful glance.

I only nodded because she didn't give me a chance to give a verbal response. I smiled as she started talking about something else. I pulled my sketches out and handed them to her.

"Here are a couple of ideas I had today about the large centerpiece you want at the gala."

While we were talking, someone paused at the doorway. He didn't knock on the door. He simply leaned in and started talking.

"I've got students who've heard about your class asking me why we aren't reading some ridiculous book that's been turned into the latest horrible Hollywood film. That's not literature, Ms. Johnston," he emphasized the courtesy title "Ms." in a snarky tone. "Stick to the tried and tested classics instead of this fluffy pop culture stuff, why don't you? They just hire anyone at this place."

` Her face had turned red as she glared at him; her eyes threw daggers as he turned away leaving her no time to respond.

"That man has all the nerve," she said as she started to count in an effort to calm herself.

"Who was that?" I asked.

"Dr. J.C. McKinney," Carolyn interjected as Gemma continued to count out loud. Once she reached 15, she took several exaggerated breaths.

"He teaches English too," Gemma growled her words in anger. "Just because he has a doctorate and I only have a master's degree he thinks he's better than I am. Fluffy pop culture? What does he know anyway? He's just jealous that students like me better."

She grinned broadly as she declared the students preferred her, and Carolyn laughed. I could see why they would. I stared at the empty doorway. J.C. McKinney was tall with dark hair slightly graying at the temples. He had a dark, short, manicured goatee and a thin beard that closely followed his jawline. From his few sentences, I could tell how arrogant he was. He had an accent I couldn't place. It sounded refined. I wondered what he was doing teaching at a two-year school.

Gemma shook her head as though she was trying to remove him from her thoughts. She took several additional deep breaths before looking back at the sketches and the photographs in the portfolio.

"These are brilliant! Simply brilliant," she said enthusiastically.

She turned her gaze back to the sketches.

"Do you need that many roses?"

"We could substitute them with something else."

"Roses remind me of home. My mother had the most beautiful rose gardens. She tried to teach me about gardening. There were so many things she tried to teach me. I even have a few of her garden implements. Imagine trying to get those through customs," she gave a weak smile. "Her green thumb did not pass down to me sadly. I kill plants, but not on purpose. My mother passed away last year, and I" -

"I understand, Gemma."

"I didn't get to say 'good-bye' in a way that I wanted. I got there too late."

She took a quick breath and started another sentence.

"Thanks for coming by, Grace. I've got class in 10 minutes. I hate to ask you to stick around, but could you meet me in the theater in about an hour? I have a couple of things I have to run by you, and I think you really need to get a look at the space to gain the right perspective."

"Of course, Gemma. I can do that."

"I'll find a place for you to relax while she's teaching," Carolyn said.

"Thanks. I do have a couple of phone calls I need to make."

There were always weddings coming up, and I had a couple of brides to run a few last-minute details past.

I followed Carolyn down the hallway from Gemma's office. On the way, we saw Dr. McKinney again. At first, he said nothing, but he began to talk as we passed him.

"You," - he said pointing at me. I stopped and turned. "You're that florist she's hired for this insane waste of time, money, and energy."

My mouth dropped. I couldn't think of a quick comeback. The sheer gall of the man amazed me.

"I "- I started to say something. I wasn't sure what it would be.

He nodded as his eyes ran over me; then a sense of revelation seemed to come to him. He started nodding as if he knew something and pointed at me again.

"I know who you are. I saw your photo in the paper along with your" - he paused and snapped his fingers before pointing at me. "Husband, was it?"

I braced myself for what might be coming next. He smirked

as he seemed to know more about me.

"Ah yes, I remember now. Let's see. You were kidnapped. Your husband, who is a police detective, shot a human trafficker to save you. Fascinating story. It would make a great play or novel. Now I know the real reason Ms. Johnston has you around," he said, once again stressing the "Ms." part. "You do know she's desperate to come up with ideas for these pathetic plays she writes. She's probably going to steal your story."

With that, he turned and walked away. I stood there with my mouth open. I must've looked like an idiot.

"He's always like that," I heard a voice behind me say.

I turned to see Carolyn. I'd almost forgotten she was with me.

"Don't feel bad. I don't know how he still has a job – period," Carolyn said motioning for me to go into an unoccupied cubicle. "You can make your phone calls in here."

"Thanks so much," I said. "He's really always like that?"

"Yes. He can't stand Ms. Johnston. I like her. She has a lot of energy and great ideas. I'm not sure what he has against her. But he's like that with most people. He's short with me, never says 'thank you' and never calls me by my name."

"He's quite rude."

She nodded.

"Grace, I was wondering if I could ask your help," she said.

"If I can, I will."

"We were talking about the camellias."

"Yes. I love them, but they aren't in season right now. She's picked the worst time of year for them."

"Indeed. Did you say you'd planted some?"

I glanced at the floor. I missed my garden and my flowers.

"My mother has bushes that are more than 100 years old. I took some of the clippings and grew a couple of bushes from them. A couple are a beautiful pale pink while the others are a vibrant dark pink. But I don't have a house now," I paused and took a deep breath.

"We sold it after my husband and I got divorced."

"I'm sorry to hear that."

I tried to smile. It wasn't as painful as it had been, but it still hurt.

"But if you'd like, late spring into early summer is the perfect time to try to propagate them. I'd love to help you."

"It would mean a lot to me," she said; her voice had a hint of sadness in it. She patted my hand and walked away.

I sat at the vacant desk, and time seemed to slip away. More than an hour passed as I worked on the last-minute changes for a weekend wedding. We were trying to avoid a nightmare. A bride learned her future mother-in-law had a terrible allergic reaction to real flowers. You'd think that would've come up sooner, but there we were. We changed the design from real to silk, and then the bride decided she didn't want the same variety of flowers. That had been a week ago. We'd been going back and forth with photos. She hated all the original flowers she ordered. She said she'd made up her mind, but I could see her changing it an hour before the wedding. Brides like this made me want to rethink my life choices.

It had been more than an hour when Gemma texted me that she had something she had to do, but to please give her another 30 minutes or so. I called Emmie to let her know what was going on and to update her on bridezilla. I was running out of busy work, so I peeked around to see if anyone was in the office. I didn't even see Carolyn. I thought I could talk with her about camellias. The hall was eerily silent. After the additional 30 minutes, I decided to make my way to our meeting point.

The theater was a 250-seat auditorium inside the information and technology building, but it would do for what Gemma wanted to use it for. Outside groups had performed plays in the theater in previous years. And it was a good reception space. It wouldn't be too hard to find because the campus wasn't that large. It was a short walk from the building with Gemma's office.

No one seemed to pay any attention to me as I walked into

the building and slipped into the empty auditorium. The lights were dimmed in the house, but there was a spotlight centered on the stage. At first, I thought my eyes were playing tricks on me. I was in a theater, after all. I didn't know much about Gemma's script, but surely, there wasn't a dead body in it. Was she working on special effects? I tried to think of anything else other than the obvious conclusion in front of me.

I walked slowly down the aisle, my stomach sinking with each step. I noticed there were a set of stairs that led from the floor to the stage wings, but I didn't have to climb them to see that my eyes were telling me the truth. There was a body, and it belonged to Dr. McKinney.

2

When I'd ended my call with Drew, I had to wait for him, alone with a bludgeoned body. I tried not to look at Dr. McKinney as I sat on the stage floor. I knew better than to touch anything while I waited. As I sat there, I'd almost forgotten about the reason I was in the theater at all until I heard a blood-curdling scream that scared the living daylights out of me. I turned to see Gemma. She'd covered her mouth with her hands and fell to her knees. I moved over to her, trying to hold her, and keep her calm.

"Gemma, it's going to be okay. I've called the police. Someone will be here soon."

It was strange to be comforting someone in this situation. Usually I was the one in need of comfort, and I probably still would be. I managed to pull up enough strength to put my arms around her as she cried.

"This can't be happening," Gemma said in a breathy tone. "Is he – is he?"

"Dead?"

"Yes."

"I'm pretty sure he is, but I'm not going to touch him."

"Who could've done this?"

"I don't know, Gemma. We have to wait here for the police."

I hugged her. I didn't know what else to do, and it seemed appropriate at the moment. She held me tightly.

A few people heard the screams and ran into the auditorium.

It wasn't long before a few campus police filed in, and then, things began to blur. Somehow, I was on my feet and heading down the stairs into the house of the theater, but there was so much confusion. I got separated from Gemma. I wanted to leave, but I knew I had to give a statement. What I was hoping to avoid was seeing Drew, but he'd be here soon enough. I sat in one of the auditorium seats. The campus police cleared the auditorium except for Gemma and me. They told the gawkers not to post any photos to social media. Like that was going to happen. I noticed one of the public safety officers talking to Gemma. I noticed her motioning to me a couple of times.

I thought about calling Trevor, but he wouldn't be able to come to me. There wasn't any point. Besides, today was one of the days he was working at the clinic. I sent him a quick text to let him know that I was okay, and if he heard anything about what was happening on the campus, not to worry.

I wasn't sure how long it took for Drew to arrive. Time seemed to stand still, and everything moved in slow motion. At one point, I looked up to see Drew on the stage, talking to the public safety officers and to Gemma.

My heart skipped when I saw him. I wasn't sure if it was out of fear or if I still loved him or if I simply needed to throw up again. He looked better than he did the last time I saw him; of course, the last time I saw him, he'd just gotten out of jail. He was beaten and bruised then. He looked healthy, and I could tell he'd upped his time in the gym. He had a few silver hairs at his temples. I'd never noticed those before. He walked over to the body and took notes before he turned his attention to me. He smiled when he saw me and began walking over to me. I remembered that smile, but instead of it bringing comfort, it stabbed me in the heart. I'd hoped some of this pain would've gone away by now. At least I didn't have to fight back any tears – yet. I tried to fake a smile, but from Drew's reaction it didn't work.

"Grace, are you all right?"

I shook my head "no."

"There's so much blood, Drew."

The words came out in a whisper. It was still hard to talk. The image of his mangled body was something I doubt I'd ever forget especially since I'd been staring at it for who knows how long.

"The human body has somewhere between 4 and a half and 5 and a half liters of blood," Drew said matter-of-factly.

"It's all over the floor up there. That's the worst one I've seen, and I thought I'd seen some bad ones, Drew. I remember why I didn't become a nurse."

"You must not remember Bill's crime scene or Jillian's. There was a lot of blood there too. "

"I only remember Dana's face and the blood on her dress with Bill, and with Jillian" -

I stopped. I didn't need to tell him that what I remembered were Drew's arms firmly wrapped around me and the way he positioned me so I wouldn't see the woman he'd shot to save my life. I couldn't look at him. I wanted this pain to go away. My voice trailed off. I couldn't complete my sentence.

"That's a good thing, Grace."

By now, other deputies were on the scene. The flurry of activity had begun. I vaguely remembered the routine. Although I'd seen it several times, I couldn't tell anyone what the police did at the scene. I couldn't pay attention to anything except for the fact that my hands, were shaking, and I still felt ill. I wanted to get away from Drew, but I had to stay to give my statement. I did at least remember that much.

"I'm going to recuse myself again from taking your statement. I'll get another deputy to do that. Okay, Grace."

"That's fine. I didn't know who to call, and I still remember your number. Funny, I couldn't remember 911, but I could remember your number."

"You did the right thing, Grace."

A female deputy walked over.

"Deputy Thompson, I'd like you to meet Grace" -

He paused without saying a last name. I wondered why. It hadn't been that long since our divorce. Did he think I'd changed it back maybe? Too much trouble. Everything was still under Ward. I stretched my hand out to the deputy.

"Ward. It's Grace Ward."

He narrowed his eyes at me and tilted his head without saying anything. As I gave my statement, he hovered nearby. He was close enough to hear everything I was saying but far enough away that he didn't interfere.

When I was finished, she walked away, and Drew walked back to me.

"Grace, why don't you sit down for a few minutes? You look really pale," he said as he led me to a chair. He disappeared for a few moments and returned with some water. I vaguely remembered seeing a water fountain and paper cup dispenser backstage. He was right. My knees still felt weak, and I could vividly see the picture of the corpse in my mind. I couldn't see the body any longer. They closed the curtains to hide the investigation from prying eyes.

Every time I thought I was getting past the disturbing images in my brain, I stumbled upon another body. Did I have some kind of dead body compass? I wasn't sure what had happened in my life in the past year that caused me to be a part of so many murder investigations. Maybe I needed to buy a lottery ticket. I had the weirdest luck.

With the curtain closed, I couldn't see what was going on, but I still could hear many voices. I'm sure they were talking to Gemma. I was in no condition to leave even though I desperately wanted to. I was already having problems. There was no way I was safe to drive. I don't know how long I sat there. I completely zoned out. That was my coping mechanism, staring into a void, and shutting down parts of my brain. I don't know how long I'd been sitting there staring at the floor on the front row of the auditorium. I heard steps coming toward me, and then a pair of black dress shoes came into view. They looked familiar. I was pretty sure I'd bought them. When I didn't look up, Drew knelt in front of me, forcing me to look at him.

"Do you think you can drive?" he asked me.

"No. My legs are still wobbly. I'm just going to sit here for a while," I said and shrugged my shoulders. "Maybe I'll sleep here. I don't want to move."

He stood up and walked back to the stage.

I did want to leave though. I didn't want to be around Drew. I hated that it still hurt. Every time he crossed my mind, I'd deliberately try to think of something else. Trevor had been wonderful, but I wanted the pain to go away. I tried to pretend it had, but Trevor knew. I still kept him at bay. I wasn't going to use Trevor as a way to ease the pain. He meant more to me than that, but I still couldn't let him in even though I desperately wanted to. I tried to stand. Maybe I'd be okay if I just got some fresh air. I went outside the auditorium. It was a beautiful March day. The pollen had already started to come. Thankfully, I wasn't allergic to it like some people. I stared at the daffodils, which were in bloom, and the azaleas, which were starting to bud.

I was starting to feel a little better when I heard a familiar deep voice behind me.

"Grace?"

There it was; that painful stab again. I turned and gave Drew a weak smile.

"Would you like to go with me for a glass of sweet tea?"

"No, I'm fine, Drew. I'll just sit down for a while. It will be okay."

He narrowed his eyes and shook his head.

"You're anything but fine, Grace."

"Don't you need to stay here and talk to people or whatever it is you do?"

I didn't want to be alone with him, but at the same time, I did. I guess it was that familiarity. I missed him still, and I really hated myself for that.

"Grace, we've been here for several hours already."

"Oh." I wasn't aware of time. Everything was a blur.

"How about I drive? I don't want to be called to any car accidents," he said and winked at me.

I think he wanted me to smile at the memory of him coming to the scene of my accident, the event that led to our eventual marriage and ultimately our divorce, but if I'd never had that first accident, my life would be completely different by now. I was sure I wouldn't be sitting here with him in a completely uncomfortable situation. When I didn't respond, he continued to talk.

"Let's take your car. Okay?"

"I'm not really sure where I parked."

"Hand me your keys. I saw your car when I pulled up."

I followed him to my vehicle. My head was screaming at me not to get into the car, but I was tired.

"Where's Emmie?" he asked after we'd gotten in.

"This was just supposed to be a meeting. No flowers. She, Jazzy, and Beth should be at the shop getting ready for a couple of events we have this weekend."

If I'd been clear-headed, I wouldn't have gotten into a vehicle with him. I was anything but clear-headed. I realized quickly that I'd made a bad decision. We didn't drive too far and pulled into a 24-hour diner not far from the campus. I knew what Drew would get – a burger and hash browns scattered and smothered. That just meant they had onions added to the hash browns. I would just get a glass of sweet tea. As we went into the diner and found an open booth, I was wondering why on earth I'd agreed to go anywhere with him.

As soon as we sat down, the waitress came and took Drew's order.

"What'll ya have, hon?" she asked and smiled.

"A hamburger, no cheese; hash browns, scattered and smothered; and some sweet tea for the lady. And make that an extra-large sweet tea for me. I need all the caffeine I can get," he said. "Are you sure you don't want anything else, Grace?"

26

I shook my head.

"No, I'm fine. Tea is fine."

After she walked away, Drew looked at me.

"You keep using the word 'fine,' but it's like I said, you don't look fine. You look green."

"I feel sick. I already threw up once. I'm not sure how you deal" -

I stopped. I knew the answer to that. I felt really stupid. My brain and mouth weren't connecting. I needed to stop myself before I said something I'd regret.

"I'm sorry," I hastily said.

"Prayer, a 12-step program, therapy, and lots of gym time, ma'am," he replied.

I glanced at him, and he smiled. I didn't answer.

"I've needed to talk to you. I just didn't want it to be under circumstances like this."

"Okay."

"How've you been, Grace?"

"Drew, you and I both know I don't do small talk. If you have something you want to say, just spit it out."

My hands were in my lap so he couldn't see me wringing them.

There was an awkward pause.

"Alrighty then," he said and sucked in a deep breath. He paused for several minutes as he seemed to be gathering his thoughts. "After the whole jail thing and stupidly putting your life in danger again, I took someone's advice and reevaluated my life's decisions."

I didn't say anything as he continued.

"A right hook from Zack helped," he said as he rubbed his jaw.

My mouth dropped.

"What are you talking about?"

I stared at him, and he lowered his eyes for a moment. He seemed embarrassed.

"Your brother decked me."

"What? Wait a minute. Zack – my brother, Zack, hit you?" I repeated slowly.

"'Hit' is a mild word for it."

"What happened?"

"The day – our anniversary," he paused as I winced at his use of that word. "After the whole Jillian thing, I went to Zack's and stayed in his garage apartment for a couple of weeks before I could find a place of my own."

I nodded and looked down. The garage apartment was my current home. It was detached from the house and had its own external entrance, so it didn't interfere with the main house. There was a small kitchenette and bathroom with a shower. It was cozy enough for one person. Not that I was there except to sleep and take a shower.

"Zack was furious with me and with good reason. He decked me," Drew continued.

"He never told me that."

"I wouldn't have expected him to."

"I'm sorry."

"Don't be. I deserve that and worse. But that was the cherry on top so to speak for the whole week. I knew I had to do something."

The waitress brought more sweet tea for him. I couldn't drink anything. He paused while she poured.

"Anything else, shug?" she asked and smiled at him.

"No, ma'am," he replied.

When she left, he started talking again.

"With Zack's help and his willingness to be my accountability partner, I started going to a 12-step program. He lets me call him whenever I need to. He's been a rock."

I just stared at him. Was it possible for my heart to sink anymore? I was glad for him, but why did he wait until now? And why was he telling me this? I glanced away as the formation of tears began to sting. I didn't want him to see me crying, and I was so tired of the tears.

He paused.

"Grace, are you seeing Trevor?"

I think my heart stopped when he asked that. In a way, it scared me. I wasn't sure why he wanted to know.

"Yes, no, I don't know what you mean by seeing. He and I are really good friends, but " -

"Why haven't you married him yet?"

I stared at him.

"It's only been three months since our divorce was finalized, Drew. That's a little soon, don't you think?"

He raised an eyebrow.

"On whose timetable? Yours or other people's? You always cared too much about what other people thought. What difference does it make what anyone thinks? You have a history with him, and I know he's in love with you. And I believe you love him too. You did before – before us. He's the kind of guy that it would probably be easy to fall back in love with. Yeah. I know that sounded weird. But I know his intentions toward you. He's the epitome of a Southern gentleman."

I swallowed and glanced down. I think I might have been blushing. This was not the sort of conversation I wanted to have with him. I fidgeted in the booth. This was uncomfortable, and I had nowhere to run.

"I'm well aware of our history," he'd hit a nerve with me. "I've lived it."

"Speaking of living. Where are you living now, Grace?"

I looked up and tried to smile at him.

"Sounds like you talk to my brother a lot. I'm sure you already know I'm at the Burke garage. I heard there was a vacancy. I travel light. I don't have a lot of furniture or things. It suits me."

He grimaced.

"And Trevor?"

"What about Trevor? Why do you keep bringing him up? He's just a friend," I emphasized the word "just." I shrugged my shoulders and stared at him. Where was he going with this?

"He's got tons of space. I've seen his house."

I held up my hands.

"Just stop, Drew. Okay. Stop. I still don't know what I did to cause you to leave me, but I'm not jumping into a relationship with someone even if that means living in a couple hundred square feet. Trevor is my friend. Just my friend."

He stared at me as I babbled on. I took a breath, but he didn't reply. I continued my rant.

"You of all people should know that I'm not going to live with any man who is not my husband. I don't care what century it is, and what the current dating rules are. I'm not doing that. Call me old-fashioned or whatever you want. It's just the way I was brought up, and that hasn't changed. I didn't live with you until after we were married, and I don't intend to live with anyone unless we have the same last name."

That came out harsh, but it was the truth. And he knew it.

"I suppose you're right about that," he said. "Like I said, I know what his intentions are, and shacking up with you isn't one of them. But there's no ring on your finger either. Why not?"

At some point, I'd stopped wringing my hands and folded them on the table in front of me. I jerked them back. Now I was getting angry.

"That's none of your business."

He raised an eyebrow at me as the waitress brought his burger. He said nothing until she left.

"Yeah, I think it is," he spoke softly.

"You and I aren't married anymore, so you don't have any say in what I do or who I see. Besides, things were moving too quickly for me, and I wasn't over you."

I think my cheeks turned a bright red when I said that. My mouth was getting me into all sorts of trouble today. I couldn't believe

I was saying all this to him, but maybe I could. We'd been married for so long I still thought I could tell him everything, but I couldn't do that.

He pushed his plate away and took a deep breath.

"You aren't sleeping with him, are you?" he asked, sounding surprised.

"Don't even go there. That's none of your business," I growled at him, emphasizing each word. "Stop it."

"I think it is, Grace."

"Oh, really. Well, you're wrong, and no, I'm not sleeping with him. How many times do I have to say this? We're just friends!"

That came out much louder and faster than I anticipated. He raised an eyebrow at me and furrowed his brow. He seemed confused.

"So, you pushed him away?" he asked.

"Yes. No. Why are you asking me all of these questions? This is none of your business."

"Because – "

He paused and looked out the window.

"Why did you leave me, Drew?"

I don't know why I asked that question. It just slipped out, like everything else. I guess I figured I'd go for broke. It jumped to the forefront of my brain the entire time I was with him.

"I told you."

"To protect me from Jillian?" I queried, staring at him to gauge his response.

He nodded slowly, but I noticed his eye twitch.

"I don't believe you."

He sat back in the booth and put down his fork. He leaned back and put his hands on his thighs. He looked outside. He seemed to be collecting his thoughts.

"I want the truth, Drew."

"I'm not sure you really do, Grace."

"That's where you're wrong."

There was another awkward, prolonged pause before he finally looked me in the eyes. He took a deep breath.

"Okay. I'll tell you the entire truth. I made the decision to push through with the divorce because of what happened that night right after Bill's death when you delivered flowers to Mrs. Blake, and you stayed in Trevor's house for several hours."

"Yeah, I remember that quite well," I snapped back at him.

"I followed you back to your shop."

"I remember that too. I also remember you accusing me of some things, Drew."

"Yeah. I apologized for that."

"I know. I'm sorry. I still can't believe you thought that though. You hadn't been gone a week, and you thought I'd jumped into bed with him. What kind of woman do you think I am? We were married still. I'd never cheat on you, and I told you everything that happened. My visit didn't center around him. I saw her. I saw his mother. The one who just died of cancer. And maybe I was wrong to have stayed to have dinner with him. But I couldn't face our house – alone."

The tears; that familiar wetness on my face. Another awkward pause. I glanced around. The diner wasn't busy at all. We were among the few people in the room, but I was having problems controlling my volume. Everyone could hear me, and they were staring.

"I'll never forget how you looked at me, Grace because it's the same way you're looking at me now."

He paused again. I'm pretty sure I knew how I was looking at him then because I'd never been so afraid of him in my life. I was afraid he might hurt me. I guess I could've had that same look. The personal questions were scaring me. I was used to prying questions from Emmie and Beth, but not from my ex-husband. I clasped my hands in my lap and stared at them.

His voice was soft as he continued.

"When I told you the whole story about Mark and Linda and why I drank, I also told you that I was becoming Mark. That night I realized just how true that statement was. The fear I saw was

32

not just in your eyes, but in your entire body. You cowered when I walked close to you; you flinched. You moved away from me; tried to put space and objects between us. Even though you were trying to be bold and stand up to me, you couldn't hide the fear in your eyes. You looked exactly like Linda did before Mark gunned her down right in front of me. Funny thing was you weren't that afraid when Jillian was pointing a gun in your temple."

He took a deep breath, and so did I.

"Somehow, I knew that I wasn't going to die by Jillian's hands. I knew you'd save me, Drew."

"Dream?"

"Yeah. I never saw how it ended, but I think I knew."

He took a deep breath before continuing.

"With everything that had happened with Mark and Linda and with us, I had a lot of anger. I had a lot of resentment and bitterness, but the hardest emotion I felt was the sense of helplessness. I couldn't give you what you wanted most in your life – a baby."

His eyes met mine with that comment, and the tears started flowing heavily.

"I was helpless to stop Mark from killing his wife. I was helpless to save Linda. I was helpless where you were concerned. I felt useless. I drank to drown out those emotions instead of dealing with them. And you realized all that. That night, standing in your shop, I felt all the jealousy and rage come to the surface. I hadn't had too much to drink. I was in control."

He paused and glanced at the ceiling. We were both uncomfortable. I didn't say anything. I let him continue.

"I'd never been so jealous, so angry, and so paranoid in my entire life. He was your first love. I knew that. I knew everything about your previous relationship," he stopped again and sucked in a long, deep breath. He shook his head before he continued. "Grace, if I continued on the same path I was taking" –

He stopped, and I just stared at him as he struggled with his next words.

"If I continued on the same path I was on, I would've ended up like Mark. I would've ended up doing what he did. It was only a matter of time. I could see why he did what he did. I felt what he felt, and I knew that if I didn't do something drastic, I'd be him and you'd be Linda. Maybe not that night, but maybe in the future. I could've done to you what he did to her."

His voice tapered off as he spoke. We were in a public place, so I tried not to react, but I'm sure my face said it all. I could feel the tears flowing. All I could do was stare at him. I saw tears course down his cheeks. That scared me more than his words because Drew Ward didn't cry.

"And I think that fear had been inside you a long time. You were afraid of me last April, the day after you confronted me about my drinking, and you left me. I broke a coffee pot, and I scared you because I'd bottled up all that anger and finally exploded. I think all of that is the reason you developed an aversion to your own gun. Why you never had it when you needed it," he said. "You didn't always hate it. We used to shoot for fun, remember?"

"Yeah, we did," my voice caught in my throat. "But, don't worry, I keep my gun close by at all times now."

He raised an eyebrow at that, but he continued.

"You were petrified of me long before either of us realized it. But that night, in your shop, I realized just how angry I really was, and it had nothing to do with you. What upset me the most was how I could be that angry and jealous. I had the restraint then. I never wanted to be one of those men I'd put behind bars. But it made me wonder. Would I have had any restraint if I'd been drunk? And I knew you wouldn't use that gun to defend yourself from me."

Was it possible to feel any worse? I took a sip of tea, hoping the sugary liquid might calm my stomach. My hands were trembling.

"I didn't do anything, Drew" I choked out the words. "I never slept with him. I still haven't."

He stared at me

"I know you didn't, Grace." he said softly. "It was me. I was the one who crossed a line that night I could never return from. I could've hurt you that night, and you knew it. When I saw you a few days later to pick up the evidence you'd found, that bloody glove of Dana's, Trevor stood between us. He was there to protect you. You had him come with you, so you weren't alone with me. He was protecting you from me. He knew it. I knew it. You knew it. I never thought anyone would have to protect you from me. I was supposed to protect you, and the only way I knew to protect you from me was to remove myself completely from your life."

I didn't know what to say. I couldn't look at him. I stared into my lap as the tears dripped onto my hands. That explanation finally made sense to me. All of the other things he'd said just never struck the right chord, but that did. I knew that was the truth that he was afraid of what his addiction to alcohol and unresolved issues could do, and so was I. I took a breath and glanced up.

"Drew, you aren't Mark. And I honestly don't believe you ever would've hurt me. You never physically hurt me before."

"No, I never physically hurt you, but I've done plenty of other damage. As much as I hate how this has happened, I think it's all for the best. I'll never be in a position to hurt you again."

There was an uneasy pause before he began to talk again.

"After we'd wrapped up Bill's murder case, Zack came to me and used some colorful language to ask what was going on. He knew I'd left you. He knew I had an alcohol problem. He knew about the PTSD. He saw all of it. He's been through similar things, so he knew me, what I was going through and what I was potentially capable of. When I told him I'd accused you of sleeping with Trevor, Zack got really angry with me. And he was right. He told me to stay away from you and that if I ever laid a hand on you, he'd gut me like a fish."

I glanced back up and stared at him. I didn't quite know how to respond to that one.

"He told you to divorce me?"

"Not in so many words, but I'd made it clear that we weren't going to work things out. He told me to be a man and do the right thing."

I didn't respond.

"Yeah. So, when everything happened at Christmas, with Jillian kidnapping you, he decked me. I couldn't eat for several days. I could've charged him with assault, but he was protecting his little sister. I deserved it. He blamed me for it all, and he was right," Drew stared off for a moment before looking at me. "I remember the first Christmas after you and I started dating, he came home on leave. He told me then that if I hurt you, he'd deck me. Since he made good on that early threat, I totally believe him about the gutting me like a fish thing. He may do it now because I've hurt you again."

Every time I thought the emotions were gone, something dredged them up. I wiped my eyes. This was not what I'd thought would happen when I agreed to have sweet tea with him.

"I want you to be happy, even if it can't be with me," he whispered. "Zack tells me that you smile and laugh a lot when you're with Trevor. He said he saw a complete transformation on Christmas day when Trevor came to dinner with your family."

"Trevor's a good man."

"He's a better man than I am."

"Drew, I've always thought you were a good man. Even though we were divorced already, I knew I had to help you at Christmas because I've always believed in you."

"I will never be able to thank you enough for what you did, never. I only hope one day I can live up to your view of me," he said. "And I can't ever thank Trevor enough either. He and I have had a couple of conversations. He picked me up when I was released from jail, and that's when he let me know he intended to marry you."

He paused, and I stared at him. I knew that was Trevor's ultimate goal. And the thought scared me. That's why I'd pushed him away. Drew tried to smile.

"Get over me and marry him. The real reason you haven't slept with him is that you are still afraid I'll hurt you if you do. You're afraid to move on with him because of me. He's not me, Grace."

He paused again. I didn't know what to say. Numbness had overtaken my body. I couldn't move.

"Grace, this is really hard. But it took me losing everything to realize that love means wanting the other person to be happy even if you aren't the one making them happy."

He stared at me and handed me a napkin to dry the tears.

"I want you to be happy, Grace. I know it sounds empty, but I do love you," he said softly. I felt like he'd stabbed me in the chest. "I probably always will, but I can't be the man you need. I proved that several times. You have so much love to give, and Trevor Blake deserves it. I don't. I want you to live a good and happy life. That's all I want for you, Grace."

"I'm sure I let you down too."

"But, Grace, when you let me down, you didn't put my life in danger. I did."

I stared at him; the tears were still streaming. This wasn't how I thought the day would go.

"Besides, I can't keep running into you like this with all these things unsaid. I just haven't been man enough until now to tell you the truth. A broken heart will heal, but I could've done damage that could never have been repaired."

I didn't know how to respond to that last part, so I diverted it. I needed to get out of this line of conversation.

"I don't want to run into you like this at all. I'm tired of seeing corpses. I don't know how I'll get that image out of my head. It was the worst I'd seen."

"Are you feeling any better?"

He had to be kidding me, right? I stared at him with my mouth open for a few moments as I tried to figure out how to answer that question. The conversation had unnerved me. I wanted to leave.

"Physically I'm not as woozy, but this conversation hasn't helped any. I don't feel well in a different way. My heart hurts a lot still."

He grimaced.

"I'm sorry," he said softly. "I didn't want to admit any of this for a while. But I had to tell you even though I didn't want to. Zack told me I needed to so you could have closure. You thought the divorce was all your fault. That's not true."

I glanced away.

"Drew, are you – "

I didn't want to know. I wasn't sure why I even started the question.

"Never mind. I don't want to know," I said, shaking my head. He raised an eyebrow at me.

"Seeing someone?" he finished my sentence. I guess he still knew me pretty well.

"Yes."

"Oh no, Grace. No way. I already ruined one woman's life; I'm not going to try that again any time soon. I'm working myself to death. Then instead of sleeping, I'm working out at the gym, spending time in prayer, and going to support meetings. I'm even going to a therapist. Something you probably should be doing. Maybe if we'd gone together things would've turned out differently," he paused and looked down. "I know you tried to get me to do that with you. I did go alone for a while when we were still married. I should've stuck with it. So many things I should've done., but like I said, it took me losing everything to realize how pig-headed and stupid I am."

I didn't say anything else; I simply stared at him. As he said that, I noticed the lines around his eyes were more pronounced. He looked so sad, so full of remorse and regret.

"Are you sure you don't want something to eat?" he asked.

"No, I don't think I could eat anything right now if I wanted," I paused and took a breath. "It's been a day."

I was ready to leave. He didn't look like he was going to finish his food, but he lingered.

"I guess this is a good lead into what I really wanted to talk to you about. Seeking forgiveness from those you've wronged is part of my process. I don't expect that you can forgive me, but I am truly sorry. And there's no way I can make amends except to push you into having a life with Trevor. I know he loves you."

I glanced away.

"I forgive you, Drew. I don't have any ill feelings toward anyone."

"Have you really, Grace?" he sounded skeptical, and maybe he was right. I wasn't sure I had even though I'd tried.

The waitress came back with the check.

"Could I have a cup of coffee please? Black," he said.

"Sure, hon. No rush on the check. Just whenever you're ready," she said.

Drew paused every time she showed up at the table. There was a long pause this time. I looked down at my hands in my lap. His words churning over and over in my brain. I glanced up to see him staring at me.

"I'm so sorry, Gracie, so very sorry. I wish I could go back and erase the things of the past that brought us to where we are now, but I can't."

I didn't respond. Hearing him call me "Gracie" brought another stab of pain.

"Grace, talk to me. Please."

"Are we finished? Can we just go now?" I asked impatiently. I wanted to go home as far away from Drew Ward as possible and cry in peace.

"No, not yet."

I took a deep breath and then a sip of tea.

"Why? What else could you and I possibly talk about, Drew?"

"Do you know anything that might help this current investigation?"

"What would I know?"

"Why were you there?"

"I went over this with the deputy."

"I know. Now, I want to hear the real story, Grace."

"What are you talking about? I told the story."

He stared at me and raised an eyebrow.

"I know you, and you never tell all of the story."

"I can't think, Drew, after everything you just told me."

"I'm sorry. I needed to clear the air."

"I'm not sure my air is cleared. My head is full of stuff now, and I'm really confused."

"I know. I'll get you back home as soon as you can tell me about the case."

I took another sip of tea.

"I do know that the woman who broke down in there – Gemma Johnston – is a professor there, and she didn't get along with the dead man, Dr. McKinney. I saw them interact this morning. He was arrogant, rude, and condescending, and she was ice cold. She glared at him. That's totally unlike her. She's usually animated and talks with her hands. She's extremely friendly – a little like Jazzy."

He laughed.

"I don't know her very well although Emmie accuses her of trying to be my new best friend. I only met her about a month ago, but we seemed to hit it off. And I met him one other time too. He's a piece of work. So arrogant. I bet there's a long list of people who'd want him dead."

"Tell me about when you met him."

"He was rude. He popped his head in her office and started ranting about her teaching style. Then, later, he passed me in the hallway," I paused. "I never thought there was any shame in designing flowers, but the way he said 'florist' made me sound like I was a drug dealer or something – like it was beneath him to talk to me. And then he implied that the only reason Gemma wanted to have anything to do with me was because of being kidnapped and you."

"Me?"

"Yeah, something about she was only using me for research for her next book or play."

He nodded and then he narrowed his eyes at me.

"Anything you aren't telling me, Grace?"

I hesitated. Was he asking if I'd had a dream? Why would he do that?

"I don't think so; like what?"

He tilted his head.

"Like a dream, maybe?"

"Why would you ask, Drew?"

I took a deep breath.

"Don't play coy with me, ma'am," he said. His tone gently mocked me. He was the Drew I remembered from so long ago.

"There was something, but it was probably nothing."

"They're never nothing, Grace."

I stared at him. He wavered on my dreams before. He'd dismissed them, made me feel like they weren't important. And now, he was asking upfront about them? Why was he doing this? Why now?

"Grace, I can never apologize enough to you about that. Your dreams haven't been evidence, but they have been keys in all my investigations. They've given me insight and caused me to look at things in different ways. Point me on the right path, please. Give me something to go on."

I eyed him suspiciously. I wasn't sure why he was prying about my dreams. I took a deep breath and hesitated.

"Today was the first day I'd actually met Dr. McKinney, so I was confused about the dream until today," I paused again as he stared at me.

"Please, Grace," he prodded.

"Anyway, in the dream, I saw her arguing with a man. I saw his dark hair. I didn't really see his face, but I know it was him. The dialogue was vivid, so real. She was upset because she read a newspaper article that talked about a play he had written and was being produced somewhere in Virginia. The story gave a brief synopsis of the play. She claimed she'd written it, and that he stole her idea. No, actually, she said in the dream that he stole her script and put his name on it. He just laughed at her, claiming she had no proof. She went on to talk about a conversation they'd had when she told him the idea in detail. He scoffed at her. He said if she tried to press the matter, he had two underage students who would claim she'd taken them out for a wild night of drinking and other activities. She was livid and threw something at him. He just kept laughing at her. I could see tears. She was so upset. She told him none of that was true. He said he knew and as long as she was quiet about the play, she didn't have anything to worry about."

"Sounds like a motive."

"Yes."

"Why are you looking at me that way, Grace?"

"What way?"

"Like you're still afraid of me."

I didn't answer right away. I glanced down. He was right. I was still afraid of him, and I was even afraid to answer that. I wasn't sure where all of this was headed. What if I said the wrong thing? I wanted to believe he could change, but he hadn't proven it to me.

"I'm not really sure what to think about you right now "

"You don't have to be afraid of me now, Grace," he said quietly. "I haven't had a single drop of alcohol in months."

"And you're not jealous now?"

It was his turn to look away.

"I didn't say that."

"Then how do I trust you?"

I stared at him and he locked his gaze with mine.

"You're absolutely right. You probably can't trust me, but I don't want to hurt you, Grace. And I value your input."

Why couldn't he have said this a year ago? I just looked down without saying anything. I forced my eyes shut to keep the tears from welling up and falling. He continued to talk.

"Any other dreams, perceptions, feelings, or conversations with Gemma?"

I snapped my head back and stared at him. I wasn't sure what to think of any of this. I just wanted to leave. I felt the tears trying to come out. This day was taking an emotional toll. I wasn't sure how much longer I could handle it.

"Stop, Drew. Just stop. You never cared before. Why would you start now?"

He took a deep breath.

"Please, Grace."

"What do you want to know? I already gave my statement."

"Yeah, but I think you know more than you're telling me."

"I'm not trying to keep anything from you."

Drew shook his head.

"That's not what I mean. I just mean that you may know something that you don't think is important but could help me."

I tried to think of anything that might help his case.

"The technical program she's trying to get started at the school. Theater has a lot of technical aspects. From the sounds of it, he's trying to take credit. I heard that from Carolyn, the administrative assistant. He'd left Gemma's name off of some of the important paperwork. Anyway, there's a gala and a play in a couple of weeks. She's trying to attract sponsors, and she's mentioned a play festival in the fall."

"How long had you been at the school before you found the body?"

"I got there around 11 because that's when she has a lunch break. She had a class at noon, but she left me around 11:45 I think. I was supposed to meet her around 1, but she texted and said something had come up. She needed a little more time and to not leave yet. I waited around until about 1:30 to go to the theater, I guess," I took a breath. "Look, I don't want to turn anyone else in who killed someone, okay? If you find out she did it, leave me out of this."

"That's not how it works. If you have information, you could be subpoenaed to testify later, and you know it."

I didn't want to be in the middle of yet another murder

43

investigation. There were a lot of things in my life that weren't going as I'd planned them.

"She seems too nice though."

"Grace, if you hear anything else, will you call me?"

I hesitated. I didn't want to call him. He raised an eyebrow at me. I simply nodded a "yes."

He paid the check and drove me back to my brother's house. We didn't talk much on the way back. I gripped my phone. I sent Emmie a text to let her know Drew was driving me home and that I'd talk to her later.

"I'm sorry, Grace" was all he said. He kept his hands on the steering wheel and fixed his eyes on the road. I tried to breathe as he drove. I watched all the signs and lights as we drove. Zack didn't live too far from my parents. He and his wife had a nice older home near Summerville. Drew was going to drive me to my brother, and Zack would ride with him to take him back to his vehicle. There was an overprotective side of Drew, and it was showing in that moment. He didn't want me to drive because he knew the afternoon I'd had. I wasn't about to argue with him. He was right. I was distracted. And his behavior was only adding to my emotional chaos. I had too many thoughts going through my head, and if he wanted to drive me home I knew better than to argue with him. There were some things you just didn't argue with Drew Ward about, and this was one of them. Zack met us in the driveway. I jumped out of my car and tried to pass him. He reached out and hooked his arm with mine so I couldn't move.

"Not so fast, little sis. Are you okay, Gracie?" Zack asked.

I couldn't say much, but he saw the tears in my eyes.

"Let me breathe for a little while."

"I'll check on you when I get back."

He let me go, and I rushed up the stairs to the garage apartment.

3

I stood shaking with my back pressed against the door of
Chateau de Burke, which was what I'd jokingly started calling the
garage. It wasn't such a bad place. It was quiet. Despite the fact that
Drew had stayed there, it didn't remind me of him. I never interacted
with him there, so we shared no common memories of the place.

. When I got inside, I sent Trevor a text. We often ate our
evening meal together. Sometimes, he cooked, but we liked to go
downtown and eat at the restaurants there. He also liked to take in
community theater productions, Fort Gordon Dinner Theater or one
of the many shows at the Miller Theater, a restored 1940s theater,
but I wasn't up to it tonight. I wasn't sure I would eat at all. I told
him I'd explain later. The conversation with Drew was unnerving,
even though he'd steered it to the investigation, I still was numb from
his words – all of them. They were too many to take in. I felt empty,
knowing that I wasn't important enough for him to get his life straight
while we were still married. Maybe that was part of it too. He didn't
love me anymore; if he had, maybe we had a chance together.

The garage had a tiny bathroom with a toilet, shower, and
sink. I needed a shower. I closed the door behind me, pressed my
forehead against it and allowed all the tears to come. I didn't have to
pretend to be strong or pretend that words weren't penetrating my
heart. I turned the water on as high and as hot as I could get it. There
wasn't much water pressure though. What did you expect? Garages

weren't supposed to have plumbing in them, were they? I cried as the water trickled down my back. I guess Drew's reasons made sense now, but could I move forward? He said he still loved me; he admitted he'd changed, that he was getting the help he needed. All the same, I realized that I wasn't enough. Part of the reason I didn't allow my relationship with Trevor to go faster was that deep down I felt inadequate. He was a doctor, and I didn't feel like I measured up to him. I guess I didn't feel like I was good enough in a lot of ways. Trevor would've told me that was stupid, so I didn't tell him what I thought.

It hurt that Drew said all those things, and he didn't want me back. In reality, I don't think I really wanted him back either, but I wasn't good at dealing with rejection. His rejection of me still stung. I still felt guilty for the divorce, guilty that I wasn't enough; ashamed of what had happened. My mind shot back to the murder. In fact, my mind was jumping all over the place. The murder, all Drew's words, Trevor and the past two years with miscarriages, death threats, kidnappings. Too much on my brain. I needed a break. I needed sleep, but somehow, I didn't think that was going to happen tonight. The sight of Dr. McKinney's bludgeoned body still made me feel sick to my stomach. Who could do such a thing? I started to shiver and realized I'd stood in there long enough for the water to start to turn cold.

After throwing on some sweatpants and a T-shirt, I walked to the refrigerator to find something that might soothe my jumbled insides. Yogurt was about the only thing in the fridge. It was blueberry and only about two days from expiring. I guess that settled it. Dinner would be blueberry yogurt.

I checked my phone. I was surprised that there were no messages from Trevor, not even one acknowledging mine. Emmie texted to check on me. I sent her a message that I was home, but I really needed a quiet night. I decided to turn my phone off. I really didn't feel like talking to anyone. The only problem with the garage was there was no porch and few windows. I wanted to sit on my porch and listen to the crickets and frogs and breathe in the spring air. But I didn't have a porch to sit on any longer. I locked the door and curled up on the couch. I had space for a couch, a bed, a small table, and two chairs. It wasn't like I had guests over, and I really only stayed in it long enough to sleep. I spent my days at the shop, ate supper with Trevor, but I came home and slept in my own bed every night. I didn't have a TV, but I did have a small library of books – mainly murder mysteries. Ironic, I suppose. I had to admit that there was something morbidly exciting about helping Drew with a case. I took a breath. I couldn't help Drew with this case, or rather, I wouldn't help Drew with this case. He needed to do this one on his own. As I was trying not to think about Drew and then relive my conversation with him, there was a knock on the door. I knew it had to be Zack. He'd gone to take Drew back to his car, and I was sure he was full of questions.

I let him in. He was still dressed in his military uniform.

"You aren't going to see Trevor tonight?"

I turned around and headed toward the couch.

"Not tonight. It's been a day," I said without looking at him.

I plopped onto the couch, and Zack sat next to me.

"I brought your car and keys back to you."

"Thanks. I probably would've been a hazard on the roadway, and there was no arguing with Drew. He was going to see that I got home safely."

"He told me to check on you when I got back," Zack said softly.

I didn't respond verbally. I pulled my knees to my chest and didn't look at him.

"I understand you and he had a long conversation," he practically whispered the words.

"I guess you could say that. He talked a lot, and I listened," I looked up at him and paused. "Thanks for decking him for me, by the way."

I tried to make it a joke, but I couldn't. Instead of laughing, I felt the tears welling up. Zack laughed for the both of us.

"That's what big brothers are for," he mocked punching me in the arm before he put it around me, pulling me out of my position. "He deserved it and more – a whole lot more."

"That's exactly what he said. Well, I'm glad you didn't gut him like a fish. You didn't need to go to jail on my account. You have a wife and family depending on you."

"Drew wouldn't arrest me for decking him. He knew he deserved it. He almost got you killed, Grace. I did what needed to be done – I got his attention. My hand hurt for several days after the fact, but it was worth it," he shook his hand as though he was recalling the pain from the punch.

He turned and looked at me.

"And there's part of me that thinks I should've gutted him like a fish for what he let happen to you," he said.

"I'm definitely glad you didn't do that. With my luck, I would've been the one to find his body, and I couldn't have handled that."

I patted his arm before I stood up and walked over to the table where I'd put my yogurt.

"It's over. I don't want to talk about it. I'm fine, and you don't have to babysit me tonight. Go see your wife and kids."

"You aren't pulling the introvert card tonight, little sis."

Zack crossed over to me.

"Zack" -

"No, Grace. No one is leaving you alone. The last time you had a really rough day like today no one heard from you for a week. You locked yourself away, and that's not happening again. You worried everyone."

He put one hand on each of my arms. His voice was tender as he spoke, and I could see that look of brotherly concern all over his face.

"Zack, that's not true. I let people know I was okay. I don't understand why everyone was worried."

"Well, let's see, your husband divorced you; you were kidnapped and almost killed; he was thrown in jail, he shot someone who was holding a gun to your head, and that was just December. Did I leave anything out? Or do you want me to go back further?"

I simply stared at him without answering.

"Plus, you have a gun, and you were depressed. And you were worried about your ex having PTSD. I don't think he's the only one who does."

My mouth fell as he said that. I stared at him as the realization of what he was saying dawned on me. I shook my head to protest.

"No, no, no. You thought I might try to kill myself?"

He nodded.

"Not me necessarily, but more than one person said it. That's why Trevor enlisted Jazzy, Beth and Emmie to do an intervention when you wouldn't see any of us, Grace. We were really scared for you. Why do you think we had Drew send an officer to check on you?"

"Mama's read too many social media posts about suicide and depression. I'm fine."

I took a deep breath, and he dropped his hands, letting my arms go.

"I'd never" – I paused. "Look, it's been a horrible day that I'd rather forget. I just want to be alone."

"Yeah, right. I know you, Gracie. You say that, but you will replay this day in your brain over and over for a long time."

"Replay which part? Sounds like Drew's already told you everything you need to know anyway. You did have some time alone with him. Besides, the two of you still are pretty good friends from the sounds of it, so why are you asking me?"

My voice rose as I spoke, and he stepped back. He held up his hands.

"Whoa, Gracie. I'm not the enemy. He's my friend in a way, but I'm not choosing him over you, if that's what you think. I've watched him punish himself as he's gone through this, and you know, there have been a couple of times when I've been happy that he's hurting. Not a very Christian thing to say, but it's the truth. He deserves some pain after dragging you into the middle of a dangerous situation. He should never have sent you that evidence. He should never have called you from jail. He opened the door for you to be taken by someone he let into your lives. He knew Butch was a dirty cop. He should've protected you from all of that instead of dragging you right into the middle of it."

"But you told him to divorce me. Really, Zack? You had no right to do that."

His eyes got big as he shook his head "no."

"Wrong, sis. That's not correct. Did he tell you I said that? I never told him to divorce you. I did tell him to make a decision and not string you along. I told him he'd better stop hurting you and to get off the fence. He decided the only way to stop hurting you was to end it all – well not really end it all, but go through with the divorce," Zack paused for a moment. "I think he regrets making that decision, to be honest. Grace, I don't know all he said to you, but I got enough from our conversation to know that you don't need to be alone right now. Like I said I can't have you pulling another disappearing act. You scared the crap out of a lot of people, namely Mama, when you did that."

"Look, I'm still trying to wrap my head around everything he said to me today. Drew told me he was afraid he might kill me one day. Is that good enough for you? Will you leave me alone now?"

His mouth dropped, but he didn't say anything.

"Yeah, Zack, that's what he said. He said he was afraid that one day it would escalate to physical violence especially if he'd been drinking."

Zack shook his head.

"No, Grace, I can promise you that if he ever laid a hand on you, I'd kill him with my own two hands, and trust me, I can do that."

"Well, you don't have to worry about that because he's doing fantastic without me. And you don't have to worry about me. At Christmas, I needed some space with everything that had happened with Drew and being kidnapped and Miss Harper's death. It was too much. I felt the world caving in on me. And tonight, I feel the same way again, but I just want to be left alone."

"But that's what friends and family are for. We push back the world that's caving inn, so you don't get buried under it. Grace, you can't push everyone away, and I'm not letting it happen again."

I glared at him.

"You've done enough. You should just go. I'll be fine. You can take my gun with you if that would make you feel better."

He folded his arms across his chest.

"Gracie, I don't care if you're mad at me. I'm not fighting with you, but I am making sure you're not going to be alone tonight."

There was a knock on the door.

"What, now? Is this Grand Central Station?" I asked as Zack walked to the door. He winked at me.

"Nope, but my relief is here."

"Who? I don't want anyone coming here. You know that."

He looked around.

"It's not such a bad place especially when it's free," he grinned at me. "And I know you don't entertain often. I think you'll like this guest."

I put my hands on my hips and glared at Zack as he opened the door. Trevor smiled as he walked in; his arms loaded with Mexican take out. Food. I probably needed to eat more than a container of yogurt. I think I was probably starving. Mexican food, at that. I could smell it. But I wasn't sure my stomach could take it.

Trevor smiled as he walked in. He furrowed his brow as Zack rushed to take the bags from him and put them on the table. Zack gestured toward me. I was surprised to see Trevor because he never responded to my text.

"Take care of her, Doc," Zack said.

"Of course, Zack. It's my pleasure," Trevor said as Zack walked past him and out the door.

"I bought your favorites," Trevor said sheepishly. "Emmie even told me to bring chocolate chip cookie dough ice cream. She said it soothes the soul."

I wanted to laugh, but I couldn't. My feet felt like they were trapped in cement. I couldn't move so Trevor walked toward me after putting the bags on the table. He wrapped his arms around me in a big bear hug.

I hadn't cried with Zack there. I'd been able to spill my anger over him. He could take it. In Trevor's arms, I felt all the tears returning to the surface. He said nothing as he led me to the couch and pulled me into his arms to sob against his chest. I thought I'd gotten some of the emotion out while I was taking a shower. Zack seemed to have opened a new vein of simmering anger. Tears seemed the best way to release the pent-up emotions. I don't know how long I cried. At some point, I could hear Trevor softly humming. Trevor told me once that he considered many songs to be prayers. They poured out of the heart in a way that only God could hear them.

He'd comforted his dying mother with the songs he sang to her, and that was his way of communicating peace and praying for her. A look of bliss came over her when he sang, even though I knew she was in tremendous pain as the cancer took its violent toll on her body. On my many visits to see her as she was dying, the music from his soul brought peace to my soul too. And now, the peace emanated from the notes; the wordless prayers from his heart. As the sobs subsided, I glanced up at him.

"Rough day?" he whispered and brushed my tears away.

I tried to laugh, but I couldn't.

"You could say that. Did you ever sing to your patients?"

He smiled.

"Only the special ones."

He moved to get up from the couch and took my hand as he led me to my tiny table and chairs.

"Why don't we eat before the food gets cold?" he asked. "And I didn't put the ice cream in the freezer. It's going to make a mess if it stays out much longer. Refrozen ice cream just isn't the same."

He unpacked the food. I knew he was waiting for me to talk, but I wasn't sure where to even begin. I didn't know what I wanted to tell him about my conversation with Drew. Drew's intention might have been to bring closure or give me peace, but none of his words did. The thought that he divorced me to prevent a murder-suicide wasn't exactly something I wanted to hear; especially when it was my murder he was trying to prevent. All of it was too much for me. I just wanted to crawl into a hole and sleep for several days.

"How did you go through medical school and see all the things you've seen?"

"I don't know how to answer that. You just get accustomed to things, and you do what you have to do. You try to save lives even though death is an inevitable outcome sometimes."

"It was a horrible scene, Trevor. It was horrible."

"Zack told me what he knew which wasn't much."

"So much blood. I can't even," I paused and looked at the food in its container. It smelled good, but I wasn't sure I could eat it even though my stomach rumbled.

"Grace, I'm not going to force you to talk to me. I'm just glad you didn't make me leave this time."

"It's nice having a shoulder to cry on. I needed that, but I feel totally spent. Zack just gave me the third degree for bottling everything up, and I let him have it too."

"He seemed fine to me," Trevor winked at me.

"Fighting is how Zack and I communicated growing up. It's our secret sibling love language. At least we don't call each other names anymore," I said and laughed. It was an empty laugh, but I was trying.

"My brothers and I never had that opportunity because of the age gap."

He started eating while I stared at the open container.

53

"How was your day?" I asked.

"Not nearly as eventful as yours."

"You seem to enjoy your days at the clinic."

"I do like working at the clinic. I like patients; I like people. I enjoyed some of my time in my oncology practice; there were just other things I didn't like. I still am not sure the direction I want to head, but my brothers have made it plain that I don't need to throw my life away as they like to put it."

He started to eat, and I watched him. The food smelled wonderful. I couldn't bring myself to eat anything. I knew he was waiting for me to talk to him. I didn't know where to start or what to say.

"Look, Grace, I won't force you to talk to me. But I didn't have a chance to eat all day. Let me eat because I'm starving, and I'll leave you alone to sleep or cry or whatever. Deal?"

I nodded. I felt a little guilty. He didn't have to come over and check on me, but deep down I wanted someone to care. He did.

"You don't have to leave right away, Trevor. Besides, you and Zack - all of you - are right, I do need someone to talk to. And you went to all this trouble."

He raised an eyebrow at me.

"You're never any trouble for me, Grace. Never."

With that, the tears started to fall again.

"You sure do have a lot of tears for a dead man you barely knew," he whispered.

I glanced down.

"I'm not a detective," he continued. "Augusta doesn't have a high murder rate. Those tears would make sense if you saw Drew today, and that he said something to upset you. I mean, you haven't spoken to him since Christmas, have you?"

I sucked in a deep breath.

"Are you sure you aren't a detective?"

"No, your brother gave me a heads-up," he said and winked.

I laughed.

"Of course, he did. It wasn't seeing Drew that was the problem. The problem came when I went with him to get something to eat. I didn't eat. I just watched him. Bad choice to go with him though."

Trevor gave me his full attention. He'd put down his fork and listened.

"No, you can still eat while I talk. You won't hurt my feelings. I'm not hungry right now, but you said you were starving," I said in protest.

He smiled at me and started to eat again.

"Drew wanted to tell me that he's gotten his life together. He's in a 12-step program and

is asking for forgiveness from people he hurt. Naturally, he wanted to talk to me," I tried to sound perky, happy. Instead it came out bitter and angry. I paused and bit my lip. I didn't want to start crying again, but it was bound to happen. Trevor waited for me to continue.

"You knew about his friend who killed his wife then turned the gun on himself," I looked directly at him when I said it.

"Yes, I did."

I swallowed hard.

"Well, Drew said he" - I paused and took another breath "Before the divorce, Drew said he was becoming Mark. He elaborated on what he meant by that today. Drew said he was afraid we'd end up like them. He said she was afraid he might kill me. Zack said he'd never let that happen, but the thought is" –

Trevor's mouth dropped, and he stared at me as I struggled to continue.

"I never thought Drew would hurt me. I mean not really."

Trevor stopped eating to reach out and touch my hand.

"He was afraid that he would kill me, kill us," I choked out the words. Saying it the second time made it a little more real. Those words stung as they came out of my mouth. I hung my head and began to cry again. I took the napkin and wiped my eyes.

"He said he's going to therapy, and he's not drinking. And he even asked me about my dreams. I don't understand. Why now? Why wasn't I enough for him? Why couldn't he have done this when we were together?"

Trevor didn't answer. He let me spill everything out.

"He said he wants me to be happy."

He squeezed my hand and gave me a faint smile.

"Was that all he said, Grace?"

"He talked for a while."

I paused. I wasn't sure what else to tell him. I moved my hands and put them in my lap I didn't really want to tell him everything Drew had said. I especially didn't want him to know the personal questions Drew had asked.

"It opened a lot of wounds. He said he knew I was afraid of him. I guess he's right on that account. I was nervous sitting with him today especially after he said he was afraid he might kill me," my voice trailed off as the thought went through my mind again. I also stopped because the realization of what I was about to say had now dawned on me. "He's staying sober now, but what if he starts drinking again? He quit before. He went to counseling before. I told him before he ever left me that I didn't want to see him destroy himself. He's done all of this before."

I stared at Trevor. I swallowed.

"And?" he asked.

I hesitated and glanced around the room.

"He pressed me about our relationship – you and me," I could feel the words tumbling out of my mouth. There would be no stopping me now. "He said that it hasn't gone any further because of him and of me being afraid of him, and maybe he's right. I think there's a part deep down in me that's afraid he'll try to do something to hurt both of us. I'd never seen him jealous before, but there was an anger and a hatred when he accused me of sleeping with you back in October. I know he's killed people – in the line of duty. He killed someone right in front of me. He's a good shot."

My voice wavered. I tried to stop those stupid tears, but I couldn't.

"Trevor, what if he tries to hurt you? He hates you. He wanted to arrest you a couple of months ago, and I think he would've found a way even though you didn't kill Bill Andrews. If Dana hadn't confessed, would he have gone after you?"

Trevor held up his hands.

"You're way ahead of yourself and Drew. Don't think about things that might never happen. It sounds like you aren't the only one who's afraid. Drew had the fear of God put in him, and that kind of fear is healthy. He took charge of his behavior because of the fear. And I think he also got a healthy dose of the fear of Zack."

He winked at me when he said that.

"You knew about that?"

"I was there."

"You were?" I asked slowly.

He nodded.

"It was that morning after he saved you from Jillian. He came to my house to tell me what had happened. Zack was there. If I hadn't been there, Drew would've had more than a sore jaw. I honestly think I stopped your brother from killing him then. Zack was furious with Drew."

I looked away.

"I'm sorry, Trevor. If you want to" -

He raised an eyebrow.

"If I want to what? Leave you?"

"Yeah. I think this is more than what you signed up for."

"Not a chance. I admit it's been an interesting few months," he smiled at me as he said that. "But I told you we'd go as slow as you needed. I told you I'd let you heal. I'm not on a timetable, Grace. I told you before that having someone who isn't after me for my paycheck or status is a relief. Women wanted to date me simply because I was a doctor and considered a 'good catch.' You knew me before I was 'Dr. Blake.' You knew 'Trevor.' I can be me with you," he said. "You aren't interested in being with me for what you can get out of this relationship. And you've given me more in these few months we've been together than I could've ever hoped. Grace, all the rest can come later. We have plenty of time for that. I know you have a lot to process. Honestly, I'm glad it's been a slow, steady friendship. You and I talk. We have fun together. This is the most genuine relationship I've had – well, since I dated you when we were teenagers. With this type of relationship, you won't have doubts about whether this was a rebound or not. I'm not leaving. I'm sorry if you think I'm pushing you into committing or being part of my life. I never meant that. I'm going through things too. I still need to figure out my career. It's been nice having someone to go through all the changes with."

"You haven't pressured me into anything. You never have even when we were teenagers."

"Then what are you worried about? You're going to let your ex-husband pressure you into an aspect of a relationship you've told me you aren't ready for yet?"

"You're right. That sounds completely insane."

"I'm glad you agree, Grace. I don't want him between us. I don't want him influencing our relationship – good or bad," he said. "Let's take everything one step at a time, okay?"

"Okay."

I didn't feel like eating much more. I got up and walked back to the couch. Trevor left his food and came to sit beside me. He put his arm around me. Neither of us said anything else. He held me, and at some point, I must've drifted off to sleep.

4

I was disoriented when I woke up around 2:30 a.m. The last thing I remembered was sitting with Trevor. I woke up on the couch with a blanket covering me and the rest of the room empty.

Since I was wide awake, I decided to open my computer to do a little research. Although I knew my dreams were real, there was still a part of me that second-guessed them and had to verify them. I thought about Gemma and the play Dr. McKinney supposedly had stolen from her. It made me curious. I pulled out my laptop and started searching for his name and the word "theater." Articles about his death popped up, but few of them gave any details about the man himself. Who was he? Where did he come from? I checked the college's website. There was a brief biography under the faculty listings. But it was just that – brief. It was odd. A few lines on where he received his degrees and nothing about where he'd taught. It only said he'd been at Tech six years.

I looked at Gemma's. It was lengthy, but that wasn't surprising since she was probably the one who wrote it. She liked to talk. I imagined her writing might be the same. Gemma's bio listed her awards; where she'd done fellowships and all sorts of details. So many details, that I was surprised her favorite food and the name of her kindergarten teacher weren't in there. This was her second year at Augusta Tech. She was quite ambitious in only her second year of teaching there.

I continued searching. And my dream didn't fail me. I found a newspaper article that was about two years old. It wasn't in the Augusta paper like I'd thought. It was from a newspaper in Virginia. It mentioned J.C. McKinney as the playwright, and there was a photo of him. He wasn't interviewed for the story; the person directing the play was. The play was about a woman dying of cancer and her quest to find the brother she never knew.

I could easily imagine Gemma writing something like that. Why would he try to steal her work? It would be hard to prove though.

His play was one of several plays that were part of a play festival. There was a cash prize for the winner. It wasn't a large prize - $500.

I kept reading; the director said the play was "touching and heartwarming," and he remarked that it was filled with "quirky, loveable characters." It sounded interesting. After meeting Dr. McKinney though, I found it hard to believe he could produce anything that was "touching and heartwarming."

I couldn't find a follow-up article to learn which play had won. Was that enough to kill someone over? I had heard of people killing for less. I tried not to think about the crime scene, but whoever killed him was filled with rage. He looked like he'd been struck with something several times. I wasn't an expert by any means, but a single blow to the head wouldn't have caused that much damage, would it? It seemed like that would take more force.

I shuddered as I thought about it.

There weren't many other references to him. Surely, he had more of an online presence than that. It was odd to me and frustrating. I wanted to know more about this man. He seemed bitter and unhappy. What made him that way? Was there some life experience or a broken relationship that caused him to be so disagreeable? I'd toyed with the idea of majoring in psychology while I was in college, but I quickly gave that one up. Minoring in English gave me enough of a glimpse into the human psyche at the time.

These murders I'd witnessed over the past 12 months had let me see too many things about people I never wanted to know.

I decided to get dressed. By the time I'd finished with my searches, it was almost five. I could get another green dragon smoothie and still have time to do paperwork before everyone came in. As I headed out the door, I looked at the clean table. Trevor had taken away any evidence of the previous evening's meal.

I was lost in thought at the shop. I tried another internet search of Dr. McKinney. This time though I did a search on Gemma. Did she have a motive? Could she have killed him? She seemed pretty shaken up when her screams filled the auditorium right after the murder. I saw her sobbing uncontrollably at one point. She was an actress. Could she fake that, I wondered. She'd be a really good one if that was the case. I wondered what Drew would say about her.

A second internet search didn't pull up much either. I did see a book that was written by him and Abigail Prentiss. It was called The Tempestuous Life and Romance of F. Scott and Zelda Fitzgerald. How did I miss that before? I wasn't sure. I checked its reviews. People were not happy with it. They called the writers "insipid" and "shallow." And they weren't impressed with the duo's writing style either, calling it "confusing" and "jumbled." As I continued to read, I found the authors' biographies. Apparently, they were married and taught together at Augusta University. The book had been published six years before. I guess that gave me a few clues into his life. I wondered what happened at Augusta University to make him leave, and I wondered if he and his wife, Abigail Prentiss, were still together.

The silence in the shop was broken by Beth as she walked into my office.

"What are you doing here so early, Grace?"

I stood up and walked back to the work room.

"I could ask you the same thing, but my name is on the building. I apologize for yesterday. I should've called you – all of you - to let you know what was going on."

"We're old pros by now," said Jazzy, who was on Beth's heels.

"What are you doing here today, Jazzy? I thought you had school."

She crossed her arms across her chest and stared at me like I had three heads.

"There was a murder on campus yesterday – of a professor. You found the body. So, the English department is closed and so are a couple of other departments. We were given a mental health day."

"Oh yeah, that makes sense. I guess I should check on Gemma."

"You should've heard all the gossip yesterday. If I believed everything I heard, I'd arrest her. She sounds so guilty."

"Really? She seems so nice. I could tell there was bad blood between her and Dr. McKinney yesterday in the three minutes I saw them together."

"Shug, there's more bad blood between the two of them than at a blood bank after a long power outage," Jazzy said with her hands on her hips.

I laughed.

"What else do you know, Jazzy?"

"Miss Grace, I could tell you tons of stories that are floating around, but I don't know what's the truth."

"Sounds like you should call Drew, Jazzy."

"Oh no, not me. I think you need to be the one to call him You were married to him."

"No, no, Jazzy. The fact that I was married to him is the reason I don't want to talk to or see Drew ever again. This is his case, and I do flowers. And I'm not getting involved this time. I'm done. That was the worst scene I've ever been to."

Beth folded her arms against her chest as she eyed me.

"The paper said it was a gruesome crime scene," Beth said.

"Gruesome is a perfect word for it. So much blood. I didn't ask how he was killed, but he was missing part of his skull" –

Jazzy put up her hands.

"Stop, right there, Miss Grace. That's enough. I don't want to know. I don't do blood and gore."

Beth put her hands on her hips.

"Jazzy's right. We don't want to know about the murder. We're more interested in something else. What happened between you and Drew yesterday?" she asked as she narrowed her eyes at me.

"What are you talking about?" I turned away to see Emmie walking in the door. Emmie leaned against the door post and folded her arms against her chest.

"You aren't getting out of it that easy. We know you saw him. He was the investigator on the scene, and we know you drove away with him and that he took you home."

"How do you know all of that?"

"We have our sources, sweetie," Emmie said.

"I don't feel like rehashing this again. I've already done it with Zack and Trevor. Did your sources fill you in?"

"Yeah, but we want to hear it directly from the horse's mouth."

"Drew's turned his life around, and everything is great in his world. He's not drinking; he's going to therapy, yada, yada."

"Well, you know the sheriff's department has recently recognized that so many of the deputies have problems with drugs and alcohol. There were five DUI arrests of deputies in like one weekend. I read it in the paper. They are making an effort to get them help."

"That's great, and I really mean that, but I don't want to talk about it."

Emmie narrowed her eyes at me.

"Oh no, sweetie, you aren't getting off that easily. You need to tell me what happened."

"Emmie, not now. I have work to do. We have a lot of things going on this weekend, and since you're all here now we can talk about flowers for the Simons-Faulkner wedding and the Matthews-Calhoun wedding. How many other weddings are there this weekend, anyway?"

"They are under control," said Beth. "They are all on the white boards in the work room. We made a lot of headway yesterday."

"Grace, have you forgotten about the authors' guild gathering this evening?"

I glanced at her. I'd completely forgotten about it.

"You did, didn't you? How did you forget that?"

"Maybe because I don't really want to see Dr. Harvey."

Beth joined in the laughter this time.

"She still wants you to write, doesn't she?" she asked.

"How did you guess?"

"That face you made was priceless, Grace. She's right though. You do have a flair for words. I've seen the sweet poems you've put on cards when the people didn't know what to say and you told them to let you handle it. You think you're being sneaky, but we've heard how those poems have touched people."

"I'm not a poet."

"You also say you don't know how to design flowers. You should just stop now. We all know it's not the truth."

"You have been looking for an outlet," Emmie chimed in. "Writing is great, and you don't need a canvas or paint. All you need is your computer or a notebook and a pen. Beth was right. We have heard comments from people who said they were really touched by the poems you've written."

"I don't know. I mean, I liked writing in my English classes at Augusta University, but I never thought I was all that great."

"You don't have to be," Emmie said. "Just do it."

"You are going with me to this shindig, aren't you, Emmie?"

"I wouldn't miss it. I love being a fly on the wall at these things. You remember she moved it this year. It's at the Partridge Inn, not her house. She has construction going on again."

"I remember. Well, it sounds like we have a full day."

"Okay. I'm going to start on the things we need for tonight. You know Dr. Harvey wants a showstopper for one of the arrangements, and I know exactly what to do. I saw it in my head last night," said Emmie. "Beth, would you like to assist on this one?"

Beth smiled and followed Emmie into the work room. Jazzy lingered though. She wasn't her usual chipper self either.

"Need to talk about it, Jazzy?"

She looked at me.

"I really like Ms. Johnston," she started.

"Come into my office," I motioned at her to follow me, and we both took a seat. "I like her too, Jazzy. She seems to care about what she does."

"She's a really good teacher. You know I'm in her class this semester, don't you?"

"Jazzy, did we talk about this?"

She nodded slowly. I paused. Just another thing I didn't remember.

"What about Dr. McKinney?"

"I've heard things about him."

"Such as?"

"He looked down on everyone especially his students. He seemed to resent teaching there. And it was so hard to get a good grade in that class. The ones who did get a good grade – well there was a joke about how to get a good grade."

"Ah. I know firsthand that he looks down on everyone, and I could see him resenting teaching at Augusta Tech. It seemed beneath him. I don't know about the other part."

"It seemed like a joke. Like they really didn't believe what they were saying anyway. It wasn't what they said but the way they said it. You know what I mean?"

"I think so. Why do you say that?"

"Well, there was one girl in my chemistry class who said he'd told her she needed to sleep with him if she wanted a good grade, but so far, she's lied about everything else I've heard her say so I don't believe her. I've known her since I started school there. But I don't know. Maybe she's telling the truth on this one."

I let Jazzy talk. She usually spoke really fast, but today, she seemed to be thinking a lot before saying anything. I wondered what was going on with her. She stopped and looked at me without saying anything. She seemed to be wanting me to say something. Her eyes pleaded with me.

"Has anyone gone to a dean or another official with any accusations, Jazzy?" I wasn't sure what to say. I'd heard about so many teachers having "improper relationships" (as the headlines always called them) with students. I didn't know what to think anymore. So many were true. It made me sick to think teachers, who were supposed to be caring for our young people were using their positions to take advantage of them.

"No, but she's really the only one. I want to believe her, but she shoots off her mouth about all kinds of stuff. I don't think anyone has really made an accusation against him. I shouldn't have said anything."

She started to walk away.

"What's really the matter, Jazzy?"

She stopped and looked at me then glanced at the floor.

"I really like Ms. Johnston," Jazzy whispered.

I got it. This wasn't about Dr. McKinney, per se. It was about Gemma. She knew something. She didn't want to say it though.

"What do you know about Gemma, Jazzy?"

Her mouth dropped.

"How did you" -

"Just tell me what you know."

She let out a sigh of relief.

"Well I got to class early a few days ago, and he was in the room talking to her. I started to go in, but they were arguing. It was something about a play he'd stolen."

Now it was my turn to stare without speaking. I took a breath. I must've made a noise because Jazzy tilted her head at me.

"What?" she asked.

"I dreamed that, and I told Drew about my dream."

She went on.

"Well I didn't hear too much, but I heard enough. She said he wasn't taking anything else of hers and claiming it as his own. He'd already gotten away with it once, but she wasn't standing for it a second time. He laughed at her, and then he walked out of the room like it was no big deal."

"She said she wouldn't let it happen again?"

"Yes."

"I wondered how many times it happened?"

Jazzy shrugged her shoulders and looked confused. I knew this meant another conversation with Drew was coming soon. It would be unavoidable at this point.

"Jazzy, we have to talk to Drew."

"I know, but I never liked him. I never liked what he did to you."

"It's not about me. It's about what's right."

"Dr. McKinney wasn't a nice man. He probably deserved it, Miss Grace. I've got more stories."

"But that doesn't mean someone has the right to kill him. I met him. I didn't like him. I've met a lot of people that weren't nice. But there are laws against killing jerks."

She laughed, and so did I.

I took a deep breath.

"Listen, I know we should call Drew, but do we have to do it right away?"

"No, Miss Grace. We don't. It's fine by me if I don't see him ever again."

I laughed.

"Thanks."

"I've got your back, Miss Grace. I can cut him for you. I lived on the streets. I do have some skills you don't know about."

"That's quite all right. My brother already promised to gut him like a fish if he hurt me again, and just between you and me, my brother hit him really hard a couple of months ago."

She smiled broadly at that.

"Good, he deserved it."

"Thanks, Jazzy."

"You're welcome, Miss Grace. Do you think she did it?"

"I hope not," I said and then I changed the subject. I didn't want to dwell on it. I didn't want to be involved. "I have a couple of baby arrangements that need to be done, and there's a funeral too. Which ones are you up for?"

"Babies," she said.

"Good, I'm going to make sure I have enough flowers ordered for this weekend's weddings."

I locked myself in my office to get paperwork and orders done while the ladies worked their magic. I was glad I had them around because they kept me on my toes. Just as I'd forgotten about the author guild and the fact that Jazzy was in Gemma's class, I'd forgotten a few other things over the past few months. I'd forgotten to place a wholesale order. I'd forgotten to pass a couple of orders along to Emmie including one for Jimmy Hughes. But Emmie was on top of things for me. She knew without saying that I was struggling. Emmie also started putting in more hours. She told me she'd help me drum up some business to earn her keep, and she'd done more than that. She came up with creative advertisements, and she'd worked a couple of booths at bridal events to get our name out there. I don't know what I would've done without her. I don't know what I would've done without all of them. I hated to be going through this, but Zack was right, friends and family were there for me to help me not feel so overwhelmed.

As I sat at my desk, several additional orders came in for the funeral of a local businessman and philanthropist. Those were the ones Beth did best for some reason, so I let her have those. The day moved by swiftly and then it was time to head to the author guild meeting.

Emmie had made one centerpiece and three smaller pieces for the occasion.

The Author's Guild of Augusta had been around since the

1920s. It started off as the Augusta Salon, a secretive gathering of literary types in the home of one of the city's wealthiest families. At meetings, they exchanged ideas and philosophies as well as shared their latest forays into poetry and prose. They still were a quiet group with membership extended on an invitation only basis. Each year, the group had a spring gathering and a holiday party. The spring gathering was just before golf week and coincided with a writing weekend at the university. A social gathering of writers seemed to be an oxymoron; most of the writers I knew were introverts, but Dr. Harvey, one of the former presidents of the group, wasn't. She had an over-the-top personality. She had taught me American literature in high school. She'd been working on her master's degree while teaching high school, but after I graduated, she went back to school for her doctorate. She was now an English professor at the university and seemed to love it. There was a poetry section in the classes and instead of writing essays, she had us critique poems and then write a few of our own. She said I had a flair for writing, but I'd never had much confidence in creative writing. She was probably the main reason I minored in English. She stoked my love of reading and nurtured my poetic side.

"So, what else happened, Grace?" Emmie asked on the short drive from the shop to the meeting.

"What are you talking about?"

"Have you forgotten that quickly? Yesterday, the murder and Drew. I was worried about you last night and you locked yourself in the office all day."

"I'm okay. Zack brought Trevor in for suicide watch duties last night, and today, I just tried to stay busy."

"What the heck are you talking about – suicide watch?" Emmie exclaimed.

"Everyone seems to think I was going to hurt myself at Christmas. Zack made Trevor come over last night because he knew that I'd spent some time with Drew."

"Well, we worried about you, sweetie. We still worry at times.

There's no denying that, but at least, you came to work today. I want to know what Drew said to you to set Zack off last night."

"I really don't want to talk about it. I'm tired of all the tears. I thought I was past most of them, and then Drew opened up all kinds of wounds yesterday."

"I get that, but what else did he say?"

I sighed.

"Can we talk about this later please?"

"You're holding things back, sweetie. I know you."

"Later, Emmie. Please. "

"Fine, but what about the case? Did he tell you to butt out like he usually does?"

"I almost wished he had. No, it was the opposite. He actually wanted to know if I had a dream about this."

"Did you?"

"Yes, I did. My dream was something about Dr. McKinney stealing a play Gemma had written. Then today, Jazzy just told me she overheard Gemma accuse Dr. McKinney of stealing a second thing she'd written. Now, I really need to call Drew, but I don't want to."

Emmie smiled.

"Hold off on calling Drew for now, but you're right, you're going to have to call him whether you like it or not. I think there could be some leads at this party."

"Why do you think that, Emmie?"

"He was an author so there's bound to be gossip."

"If there's gossip, then you can call him. I'm not helping Drew. I should've called him earlier because of what Jazzy knows, but I just can't. That's over. After yesterday – "

I could feel the tears stinging.

"What happened, sweetie?"

"I'm five seconds away from a major meltdown, Emmie. Please don't ask me again. Not now."

"I'm sorry, sweetie, but if you don't want to talk about it so badly, then why do you keep bringing it up."

"You're right, Emmie. Later."

I'd almost wished the gathering was at Dr. Harvey's home in Summerville. The one thing I loved about Summerville was the different architectural styles of homes. Hers had a hodge-podge of different styles, but there were definite Queen Anne influences with its balustraded front porch that wrapped around a two-story turret. It had been vacant for several years before she and her husband restored it. When she wasn't teaching, she spent her time renovating her home and showing it off to her guests. She'd even put it on the neighborhood's annual tour of homes a few Octobers ago. I'd helped create arrangements for every room. I'd used some of the flowers in her garden in some of the creations.

She had a beautiful garden, but she still called on me from time to time to bring flowers to her events. I wasn't sure if she pitied me or what was the reason she called. I was always grateful someone did.

Instead, she'd booked one of the conference rooms at the Partridge Inn for this gathering. The Partridge Inn was just down the street from her home. It was originally built in 1816 as a two-story residence for George Walton, one of the three Georgia signers of the Declaration of Independence. It remained a residence for many decades before it was purchased by Morris Partridge in 1892.

Because of Augusta's mild winter weather and because it was at the end of the train routes until the 1930s, many wealthy Northerners spent winter months in Augusta. Mr. Partridge was a hotelier from New York, and he turned the residence into a 60-room hotel. It was only a few decades, however, before Florida became the southernmost destination for wintering Northerners. Augusta was bypassed and the Partridge Inn fell into disrepair. Like many Augusta landmarks, it faced a wrecking ball in the 1970s when a lawyer purchased it. It was restored and later purchased by a large hotel chain, which has kept it in operation since.

It's on the edge of the Summerville neighborhood and sits at the crest of the hill on Walton Way named after George Walton. The inn has beautiful porches and one of the best views of Augusta from its rooftop bar. You can see for miles perched atop the hotel. It's truly breathtaking.

The Inn is a popular spot for weddings and receptions. There's even a ghost named Emily who supposedly haunts the place. According to folklore, Emily was one of the Inn's brides in the late 1800s and was in the middle of donning her dress when she received word her fiancé was shot and killed. She never married and is said to walk the halls of the inn in her wedding gown. I've done quite a few weddings and receptions at the Inn, and I've had a couple of brides tell me after the fact that they saw her on their wedding night and were petrified.

To get to the parking deck, we passed another glorious building across the street from the Partridge Inn. The Bon Air Hotel was built in 1889, but it was destroyed by a fire in 1921. It was rebuilt in 1924 as the Bon Air Vanderbilt Hotel, and I've heard it was majestic in its day. It's listed on the National Register of Historic Places. It was a premiere hotel which once housed numerous conferences and dignitaries including President Eisenhower's press corps and staff. Eisenhower loved Augusta. He frequently played golf at the Augusta National, where he was a member before he became president. There was even a loblolly pine on the National's 17th fairway named after him, but Pax, the terrible ice storm of 2014, damaged the tree, and it had to be removed.

The Bon Air's most recent use has been as housing for low-income senior citizens. From the outside, you can see glimpses of its former glory days. Unlike the Partridge Inn, the Bon Air is in need of renovations, but I'm sure that would cost a pretty penny.

The Partridge Inn has a ballroom and meeting spaces of different sizes. For this gathering, we were in one of the smaller rooms.

When we pulled into the parking deck, Emmie paused before turning off the vehicle.

"Are you going to be okay, sweetie?" she asked.

I took a breath.

"I'm fine, Emmie."

"You look like you're on the verge of tears again"

"I can hold it together. We won't be here long. Just don't ask me about Drew again."

"Are you sure about that idea of leaving quickly? The last time you brought flowers to the Author's Guild, Dr. Harvey wanted you to meet a few people."

"Yeah, she still raves about those poems I wrote in high school. She's been after me to submit something into that literary competition. That's one of the things they announce the winners of this weekend, you know."

"I remember. She always had a soft spot for you."

"I know. I never understood that."

Dr. Harvey was waiting for us as we unloaded the flowers.

Emmie and I took in the largest one first. As usual, Emmie had knocked the design out of the park. It was beautiful and smelled incredible.

"Oh, this is perfect," Dr. Harvey exclaimed. "I love it. Grace, you've outdone yourself."

Emmie winked at me as we moved away from the room's main table. The room was set up for a reception. There were a few round tables in the room, and one large table for the hors' d'oeuvres. the chairs were closer to the walls. There wasn't really going to be a meeting, and it wasn't a dinner, so everything was in an informal layout. There were two additional arrangements.

After we'd brought them in and she'd configured them the way she wanted to, she grabbed me by the hand.

"Now, you are staying tonight, aren't you?"

I opened my mouth to say "no," but she patted my hand.

"Wrong answer, Grace, I have a few people you need to meet."

I could see Emmie, winking and giving me her famous "I told

you so" look, but before Emmie had a chance to escape, Dr. Harvey turned her attention to my friend.

"Emmie, I heard about your art exhibit at Grace's shop at the beginning of the year. I'm sorry I missed it. I was out of town that weekend. You will have to do it again."

Emmie smiled.

"The next one is at the end of next month," she said.

"I'll be there," Dr. Harvey said and smiled. "Emmie, could I borrow Grace for just a moment?"

Emmie nodded.

"Of course."

"Just make yourself comfortable for a few minutes."

She led me to a corner of the room.

"How have you been, Grace?"

"I'm well."

"Are you? Have you written anything lately?"

I wasn't sure how to answer that. I'd thrown jumbles of words onto a page, but they were just that – jumbles of words with no rhyme, no reason, no flow.

"I sometimes write poems to go along with arrangements."

She grinned.

"I love that, but that's not what I mean. I've kept up with you through your mother. She and I see each other the first Thursday of each month at the Kings Way Market social. I love getting antiques and paintings from there."

I stared at her.

"You mean to tell me my mother discussed my personal life out in public?"

She laughed.

"No, no, nothing like that. We talked at her car," she said winked. I wasn't sure that made me feel any better. I glanced down. "She is adamant about keeping your reputation cleared, so you shouldn't feel badly."

I didn't say anything.

"But that's not what I wanted to talk about with you anyway. I want to hear about your writing. There was a spark in your words."

"That was so long ago. I haven't written anything anyone would want to read."

"When you get my age, 15 or 20 years seems like a blink. Besides, it's not necessarily about publishing. I read the paper; I hear the gossip. And I know one thing. I know that writing brings healing to the wounded soul. You can pour your soul out to the page and not worry because the page will never judge you."

I glanced down uncomfortably I thought I might tear up with those words. I'd felt a lot of judgement, especially at Trevor's mother's funeral before Christmas. I knew what people thought, and I still didn't think Trevor's brothers approved of me.

"Thank you."

"Grace, I was at Mrs. Blake's funeral. I saw how uncomfortable you were," she said; her voice was hushed.

I looked up to see her smiling kindly at me.

"He's just a friend."

She continued to smile.

"I remember how you looked at him when you were in high school. I saw the two of you together then. You wrote some amazing poems in high school. They were full of love, so beautiful. And despite being uncomfortable in the surroundings in December, you still had that look when I saw you at the funeral. He seemed to draw strength from you being there."

"You just observed all of that?"

"Yes. I read people, just like I read books. I'm right a lot of the time. I'm not judging you. Your mother has set the record straight. What I can tell you is that the emotions that come from personal tragedy and love are great forces when it comes to writing, especially poetry. They stir up all kinds of words that are waiting to get out. And you are full of unspoken words. You missed this year's competition, but who knows? Maybe next year?"

I tried to smile. She simply patted my hand.

"I have thrown a few things down in my journals, but they mean nothing."

"No, Grace, they never mean nothing. They are the reflection of your soul. Bring them to me sometime. Let me see them."

I swallowed.

"I don't know."

She smiled and squeezed my hand.

"That's okay for now, but I do want you to meet Lucinda Clark tonight. She publishes poetry and has several poetry groups that meet regularly and hold open mic nights at the Book Tavern. You might not want to do anything with them now, but I want to open the door to you. Besides, you have a great spot in your shop that could be used as a gathering place if you're so inclined. David at the Book Tavern is great, but he has so many events there. It's hard getting on his calendar."

I smiled.

"Grace, there's another reason I wanted to pull you aside. Your mother told me that you had helped Drew on a few of his investigations."

"I'm not sure that's what he'd call it. Meddling, interfering, getting in the way, maybe. He was never really happy about it."

She smiled.

"I guess you heard I found Dr. McKinney's body, then?"

"Yes, indeed. That is the rumor floating about," Dr. Harvey replied.

"Was he a member of the guild?"

In the author's group, there were writers from academia and other walks of life. They wrote all kinds of works from contemporary fiction to poetry to articles for academic journals. There were a few journalists and one of Augusta's former mayors in the group.

She laughed at my question.

"He was. Authors can be pretentious people, and if ever there was an example of that, it was J.C. McKinney. He was every bad author stereotype there ever was," she said. "But honestly, his biggest stereotype was of melancholy poet."

"Really?"

"Oh yes, he was married to our incoming president at one time," she said. "But they divorced a few years ago."

"Would she want him dead?"

Dr. Harvey pursed her lips.

"There were lots of rumors about the two of them, but to be completely honest, I was surprised when Abigail divorced him."

"What were the rumors?"

"Oh, the usual. Infidelity, emotional abuse. With them, there was a competitive spirit.. She really rubbed his nose into the fact that she was published more."

"Doesn't sound like a very healthy relationship."

"And that's why they are no longer in one. They simply called it 'irreconcilable differences.' The two of them were quite strange. He'd taken a leave of absence for a semester and when he returned, they divorced quickly. Only people close to them really knew how competitive they were with each other. They hid things very well. But when she left him, it devastated him. He even quit the guild because of her. I always thought she gloated a little too much where he was concerned. I believe in women succeeding in things and being celebrated as much as their male counterparts, but like I said, theirs was an odd relationship. Quite honestly, I think she sucked the life out of him."

"Dr. Harvey, why did he teach at Augusta Tech? I mean it's not a place for someone with a PhD in English to teach. They only do introductory English classes there."

"I never knew the answer to that question because he did teach at Augusta University at one time. There were rumors there too. I even asked him a few times why he'd left the university. He never answered. He would just glare at me with one of those 'it's none of your business' kinds of stares, and he'd move on."

"How long had he been here?"

"About seven years I suppose. Abigail suggested him for the

guild. They were married when they both moved here."

"Where did they come from?"

"My, all the questions, Grace," she said and laughed. "They came from Colorado."

"Where did he go on his leave? Or do you know?"

"Rumors were that he was teaching a theater workshop in Virginia."

"Theater?"

"Oh yes, he was really involved in theater in Colorado from what I understand, but he left all that behind when he went to Tech."

That would be a reason to hate Gemma.

"You think his ex will be here today?"

"Oh, I do. I think it would be her ultimate way of rubbing it in and letting him know she'd won."

"How do you know all this?"

"Watch and listen, Grace."

"You sound like Trevor."

She smiled.

"Guild members should be arriving shortly, but remember, don't leave."

I watched her as she sauntered out of our corner. She seemed to float when she walked. Her feet barely touched the floor and made no sound as she breezed out.

I followed her slowly and found Emmie moving a few stems around. That was her way of trying to look busy. She saw me coming and caught my eye.

"So, are you going to trade your sketchbook for a leather-bound journal for all that poetry you're going to start writing?"

"I'm a woman of many talents, or didn't you know that?"

She put her hands on her hips and raised an eyebrow.

"I don't know why you are always putting yourself down. I thought Trevor had pulled you out of that."

"He's tried."

I looked around the room. I wanted to go, but part of me was curious. Emmie seemed to sense my hesitation.

"Did Dr. Harvey talk you into staying, or do you want to leave?" she asked.

I didn't look at her. I watched as a few people milled in. I wondered what Abigail Prentiss looked like. I was interested now. I wanted to be a fly on the wall to see how she reacted, to listen if she said anything unusual.

"Not yet, Emmie; not just yet."

Emmie's eyes twinkled as a huge grin spread across her face. I eyed her suspiciously.

"What?"

She smiled even bigger if that was possible.

"You."

"Me what? Talk to me, Emmie. Don't be vague."

"You're back, sweetie. You have that look."

"What look?" I was getting aggravated with her.

"You have the 'I'm going to solve Drew's case no matter what he says' look."

"I didn't know there was such a thing."

"Oh yes, hon, and you're doing it right now. This is great. I've missed this so much."

She winked at me.

"I've already told you. I'm not helping Drew. I just want to see if anything interesting happens when his ex shows up."

"Yeah, sure, and I'm the Queen of England. I bet Beth would love being a fly on the wall with us. Maybe I can call her so she can listen in."

I shook my head at Emmie.

"You're incorrigible. You do know that."

"Oh sweetie, you have no idea, and you're going to figure out how to help Drew whether you want to or not."

I glared at her while she laughed at me.

"Dr. Harvey is pretty sure she's going to be here, and she did invite me to linger."

We found a spot in the corner where we could be out of the way, but where we could watch everything at the same time. The reception started around 5, and it wasn't long before people began to arrive, and Dr. Harvey made her way toward me. She was talking with another woman.

"Grace, this is Lucinda Clark; this is my friend and former student, Grace. She's a poet, but she doesn't give herself credit. I told her about your group and your events."

"It's nice to meet you. We'd love to have you come to one of our open-mic nights," she said.

"Thanks. I'm not very good."

"If Dr. Harvey thinks you're good, then you are. I'd love to talk to you about poetry. There are contests and ways to publish your poetry."

"Oh no. My poetry is just for me but thank you."

"Here's my card. If you need anything, let me know."

I smiled. I didn't know what to say. I don't know why Dr. Harvey always made such a fuss. She walked away and began talking to someone else. I strained my ears for other conversations. I hadn't heard anyone mention Dr. McKinney, but it was early still.

Emmie fidgeted when she was forced to wait. She had little patience. It was worth the wait though. Around 5:30, Dr. Prentiss finally made her appearance, and what an appearance it was! She was drunk and stumbled into the room with flair. I had my phone out and snapped a photo. I hoped no one saw me do it, but I needn't have worried. All eyes were on her.

Dr. Harvey rushed over to help her in the door as she wobbled and nearly tripped on the carpet. Dr. Harvey helped her to a chair.

"I'm fine. Totally fine," she slurred her words and waved her hands to shoo her handlers away. "Now that he's dead – all is right in the world."

I glanced at Emmie.

"I'm sorry, sweetie, but you're going to have to talk to Drew now," she whispered.

"No, not happening. You know his number. You're a witness to this too."

Several people swarmed around Dr. Prentiss. I'm not sure if they were trying to protect her or get a closer look at her. There was a low rumble in the room as people talked amongst themselves about her, but I couldn't make out what they were saying. I could only understand her periodic outbursts.

"He deserved it after what he did," was one of the phrases I'd heard. I surreptitiously videoed the scene on my phone as Emmie eyed me and smiled knowingly. "You all know he did."

It didn't take long for them to usher her out of the room.

I wondered what she was talking about. Dr. Harvey had mentioned infidelity. And I wondered what it was about Virginia. That's where he'd gone on his sabbatical, and that's where his play was entered into the contest.

Within a few minutes, Dr. Harvey had returned to the room.

"We're going to continue with the reception, and we'll hear from our president another time. In the meantime, please make sure to pay your dues and sign up to volunteer for the book talks we'll be having in the fall. We need to start planning those soon."

I exchanged glances with Emmie. She nodded and smiled. We'd known each other long enough to read each other. She wanted to linger to hear what people would say about the outburst. It wasn't such a horrible idea. I couldn't deny there was a part of me that wanted to throw myself into Drew's investigation. I just couldn't figure out how to do that without running into Drew again. Maybe I could simply have the satisfaction of knowing who killed him before the newspaper reported it. I could tell myself that, right? Besides, I knew Emmie was chomping at the bit to learn more about the murder too. Since her temporary contract with the FBI had ended, she seemed lost at times, and she knew way too much about serial killers like Ted Bundy from the documentaries she'd been watching on TV. She enjoyed crime-solving, and I was sure she'd try to find her way back into the mix of it.

"Well, Dr. Harvey did tell you to stay around," she said and shrugged her shoulders. "Besides, you know you don't want to leave when it's finally getting interesting."

"That she did. We can eavesdrop for a little while and see what happens."

Members of the group stood in stunned silence for a few moments before the whispering began. They all seemed to have theories as to what exactly Dr. Prentiss meant.

"I heard he had an affair, and that's the reason they divorced" was one of the comments I overheard. Others pondered out loud if he'd ever assaulted any of his students. Maybe that's the reason he deserved it, they mused. Others chimed in that they never really cared for him. They wondered how he got a doctorate because his writing wasn't up to par. And still another echoed Gemma. One of the women said she heard he'd plagiarized his work and that's how he got as far as he did.

We tried to be inconspicuous, and we retreated to a corner not too far from where a middle-aged balding man and a silver-coiffed woman were talking. We weren't standing too close, but we could hear everything they said. I was just about to signal Emmie to let her know I was ready to leave when something he said piqued my interest.

"You know he has an adult daughter," he said.

"Really? He was married before?" she responded.

"No, it was a fling. From what I gathered, the daughter lived in Virginia, and that leave of absence he took a few years ago was to mend the fences. But something happened there. No one knows what. When he came back, Abigail had already started the divorce process."

"Where's this daughter now?"

"I have no idea," he said

"Why have I never heard any of this before?"

"I guess some people keep good secrets. You knew he had a

nom de plume, didn't you?"

"Not surprising. A lot of us in this room do. I would love to check out his writing. Could it be as awful as the book he wrote with Abigail?"

He laughed loudly.

"It was positively dreadful."

"What was his name?"

"James Mitchell."

"How did you find that out? He was secretive about everything," she said.

"I have my sources. I tried to confront him about it, but he denied it. He said he'd never heard the name. He was super nervous. I thought I saw beads of sweat break out over his forehead. He looked flushed and quickly changed the subject. To be honest, I don't think J.C. McKinney was his real name. I always thought something was off about him. He had lots of secrets. Some we'll probably never know the answers to."

"Then how do you know it's him?"

"I was in his office another time, and I saw several books written by James Mitchell. They weren't polished books by any means. It looked like an amateur cover on the books, but the author name was plainly James Mitchell. I thought it was odd. I asked him about them. He tried to hide them from me. He picked them up and put them in his desk drawer. Then he brusquely asked me to leave. I never saw the books again."

I leaned to whisper into Emmie's ear.

"Have we heard enough?"

"I doubt it, but let's walk toward the door. I wonder where they are keeping the ex-Mrs. McKinney?" she asked.

"Maybe we can see her on the way out," I said as we slipped out the door.   I wondered about this new name of his, and if he ever used it for anything besides writing. I was curious about that. It could open up a whole new avenue.

We found Dr. Harvey, Dr. Prentiss and another woman in

the parking area. They were insistent that Dr. Prentiss leave, but she wasn't driving anywhere. She was quite loud about her desire to stay.

"How did you even get here without killing someone or yourself?" Dr. Harvey asked.

"I have no idea," Dr. Prentiss slurred her words.

"You aren't getting out on Walton Way. That one curve out front will kill you or somebody else," the other woman said. "I'll take you home, Amanda."

"I can't believe he's gone. He's dead. It shouldn't surprise anyone. The truth will come out," she rambled.

We got in the car slowly. I rolled down the window to eavesdrop just a little longer.

"Why do you keep saying that, Amanda?" Dr. Harvey asked her.

"He hurt people. He hurt a lot of people over the years. Why did it take so long for this to happen? I should've done it a long time ago."

With that, Dr. Harvey pushed Dr. Prentiss into the vehicle and slammed the door. I turned to Emmie.

"Okay, sweetie, you and I need a girls' night tonight," she said. "I'm going to call Trevor and tell him you're mine tonight. I don't have the boys, so I'm alone, and you need death by chocolate because you have a lot to tell Drew."

"Fine."

She laughed.

5

I let Emmie do the ice cream shopping. I needed some poster board and some sticky notes and different colored pens. I wondered about that supposed pen name. What kind of secrets did J.C. McKinney or James Mitchell take to his grave? I stared at the office supplies as all kinds of thoughts rolled over in my brain. I held the poster board in one hand and a small basket in the other. Emmie strolled up next to me and smiled. Chocolate chip cookie dough ice cream, chocolate syrup and chocolate-covered almonds were in her basket.

"Uh-huh," she said as she looked in my basket.

"What?"

"I thought you weren't going to help Drew."

"I'm not."

"And that's why I said, 'uh huh.' I know you, Grace Ward."

I smiled at her but said nothing.

Once back at her house. I started writing down our list of "suspects" along with their possible motives and the opportunity. Emmie brought in two bowls with two heaping spoonful of chocolate chip cookie dough ice cream drowning in chocolate syrup.

"I haven't done this in months, Emmie. I might get sick."

I tried not to laugh.

"You mean the ice cream or the crime solving?"

"Both I guess."

"Well, you're the boss. You can call in sick if you need to, remember?"

"I'm not eating all of this."

"Yeah, yeah, sure, sweetie. So, what are we watching tonight? We haven't had a good movie cry in a while."

"Let's not start back. I've cried enough in real life."

"I know, but when you cry over characters, it's different. You know that, Grace."

"I'm in no mood to cry. I need something ridiculously and stupidly funny."

"How about The Money Pit?"

"That works. I don't know why I still laugh at that cheesy movie, but it's funny. Tom Hanks in the carpet in the ceiling and that turkey flying through the air. So hilarious."

"Perfect. I'm glad I kept my obsolete DVD player."

She got up and put the disc in the player.

"So, Grace, what are you doing if you're not helping Drew?"

"Well, I'm going to make a chart of suspects with motives and everything we know about their alibis. and we'll all chip in $10 and draw a name. The person with the right answer will get the pot," I glared at her when I said that and my sarcasm wasn't lost on her.

She raised an eyebrow as she folded her arms across her chest.

"Try again, sweetie. Like I believe that. You are not the lottery pool type, and you know it."

"Then why are you asking me? I don't know if any information I have will help him, but I want to organize it all in one place. Besides I sure would like to figure out what's going on, and I know you would too. The disgruntled English professor, the bitter ex-wife, possible abused students, an estranged daughter. And what do you make of that new name? I wonder if that's true. You know I tried to find out things about J.C. McKinney on the internet, and my search came up short. I thought it was really odd considering who he was. I would've thought I could've at least found a bio. He's written some books. Surely he has some type of digital presence."

"I'm sure you're right, but you should share what you know with Drew."

I glanced away and took a deep breath.

"I was supposed to call Drew for Jazzy, and I didn't do it."

"Grace, I can forgive the rest, but not that. If Jazzy has info, you're going to have to coax it out of her, and you know it. It could be something that would help. I don't want Drew dragging you to jail because you didn't help him. And we have to tell him about our eavesdropping adventure."

I knew she was joking. She grinned her best "Emmie cheers up Grace" grin, but it wasn't working.

"Emmie, don't you get it? I don't want to see Drew anymore. I want to get over him. I want – "

I paused and looked away.

"No, sweetie, you can't just stop there."

"I want to move on with my life. I want to have a life."

"With Trevor?"

I didn't answer right away. Instead I looked away from her prying gaze.

"Coming over here tonight wasn't a good idea, Emmie. I need to go home."

"Not so fast, sweetie. I'm your best friend so I want what's best for you, and you know it.

Will you please tell me what happened last night?"

"We have a case to solve, and I want to do a search on that new name."

"It can wait, Grace. Talk to me."

"It's like I told you earlier. Drew has pulled his life together – 12-step program, counseling, no alcohol, diet, exercise and prayer. He's doing fantastic. He divorces me, and now his life is wonderful."

I slouched back into the couch.

"Uh huh. Somehow, I doubt his life is wonderful," she said and pursed her lips. "What else, Grace?"

I glanced away from her.

"I've already gone through this with Zack and Trevor."

"Grace Burke Ward, we made a pinky promise in 4th grade that we'd share all of our secrets with each other, and you know it. Nothing held back."

I took an exasperated breath.

"Fine."

"That's better. I like the attitude."

I didn't know where to begin, so I decided to jump into it.

"When Drew left me, he'd said he was becoming like Mark."

"Yeah, I remember you saying that."

"Well, he said he could really see himself becoming like Mark – how Mark was at the end. And if Drew didn't stop drinking, he was afraid we might end up like them."

She narrowed her gaze at me. It took her a few moments before the meaning dawned on her.

"Wow. Wait a minute. He thought - Drew never physically abused you before, did he?"

"No, he never hit me, but Mark didn't just one day shoot Linda and then himself. It built up over time, and Drew said he thought that with enough alcohol, enough jealousy, enough paranoia and – " I took a breath. I couldn't keep saying it. I didn't want to hear it from my lips again.

"He was jealous of Trevor."

"Come on, Emmie. You know he was. I didn't do anything, but you know what he said to me. I guess I opened a door I could never close. He saw what he wanted to see between Trevor and me. He jumped to conclusions early on. Anyway, he felt that he might" - I paused. "You know he saw a lot of domestic violence, and so much of that came from alcohol and drug abuse."

"Grace, exactly what did he say? All of it. Stop dancing around it."

I winced.

"He thought he was capable of murdering me and killing himself if he drank too much. There, that's what he said to me."

She stared at me for a minute.

"Is he still jealous?"

"I'm pretty sure he is, but at the same time, he told me he still loved me. And he said that he wanted me to be happy even if it wasn't him making me happy."

"Wow. He's all over the place, isn't he, Grace?"

"Yeah, he is, but Trevor and I aren't a couple. We're just good friends. People probably think other things. Honestly, I've been afraid to let things happen between Trevor and me. I'm afraid to let him kiss me. He has, but not since New Year's Eve. I told him I didn't want anything physical between us. I couldn't handle it yet. I told him I needed to build our friendship and make sure it was solid before anything else happened. Besides, I still have this crazy mix of feelings towards Drew. I still think about the way he touched me, and until I stop thinking about that, I can't be with Trevor. It's not fair to Trevor. My heart skipped when I saw Drew come into the theater."

"Are you sure that wasn't a panic attack coming on?" Emmie quipped and then smiled.

I laughed nervously.

"I guess that's possible, but if I'm still in love with Drew, I can't have a relationship with someone else. Besides, I'm still afraid of screwing up a life with Trevor."

"How many times does your ex-husband have to tell you it wasn't anything you did?"

"I don't know, but I did tell Trevor if he didn't want to be with me, I understood."

"What? And what did Trevor say to that?"

"He said he wasn't going anywhere and that he understood I needed to work through this."

"I know we've given you a hard time about Trevor. He really does care about you in ways I don't know Drew would've even thought of."

"Yes, I want to have a life with Trevor. He's amazing, but Drew could be right. Am I afraid of him? I wavered on that. There were times when I didn't think he'd ever hurt me, but there were other times when I wondered what he was capable of. I mean, I was standing inches away from a woman he shot and killed. He's got it all together right now, but you and I both know, he hasn't always followed through. Trevor said not to worry about it. How can I not worry?"

"Oh, sweetie," Emmie said as she put an arm around me. "Everything's going to be okay. You can't live your life in fear. And you can't push the pause button on it either. Drew's made it clear he's not coming back. I know you still love him, but I also know that you have really strong feelings for Trevor that you don't want to admit. And you seem to think everyone is judging you. Who cares what they think? We have done flowers for weddings for people who got married the day after a divorce was final. You never judged them. You only smiled and wished them happiness. If people can't do that for you, they don't need to be in your life."

I glanced at her.

"Thanks for the pep talk."

"It's not a pep talk, hon. You know it. If you don't want to take my word for it, why don't you talk to someone else? Like Pastor B or any of the staff at church. You went to counseling with Drew. You tried. You gave it your all, but you can't force someone to try to make something work if they don't want it to. And you couldn't make Drew stop drinking. It was all his choice."

"I know. He chose that over me. I wasn't good enough for him to stop doing it while we were together. I don't want to talk about this anymore. I want to play 'who killed the professor?'"

Emmie laughed.

"I'll let you off the hook for now, but I'm not finished with this subject."

"I know how you feel about Trevor, Emmie. You, Beth and Jazzy have made it clear. Trust me. You'll be the third to know if anything happens."

"We all know it's not an 'if,' but a 'when.'"

"Fine. When."

I knew I needed to call Jazzy. She had a few other suspects for us to put on our list. I dialed Jazzy's number, and she picked up right away.

"Miss Grace, did you ever call Drew?"

"No. That's the reason I called."

"Well, I've got more info than you could ever want to hear. Are you at Miss Emmie's?"

"Yes."

"Save some ice cream for me. I'm on the way."

"Do you have another bowl," I asked Emmie as I put my phone on her table.

"You betcha."

It didn't take Jazzy long to arrive. She knocked, but before we could tell her to "come on in," she was already in and making herself comfortable in one of Emmie's chairs. Beth followed closely behind her.

"What is this, Grand Central Station?" Emmie asked.

Beth mocked being offended and folded her arms across her chest.

"You and Grace have all the fun. I'm tired of hearing about all your 'death by chocolate' experiences with movies all night. I want a girls' night too," Beth said with a fake pout.

"What kind of ice cream y'all got?" Jazzy interjected.

"Chocolate chip cookie dough with chocolate syrup," Emmie answered. "Do you want some too, Beth?"

"You'd better believe it," Beth said.

Beth followed as Emmie headed into the kitchen. They emerged with the container of ice cream, bottle of chocolate syrup, bowls and spoons.

As Emmie scooped the ice cream, Beth leaned over.

"I thought you didn't want to help Drew," she said and raised an eyebrow at me.

"You sound just like Emmie. I'm just putting a puzzle together.

And I think we'll have a pool. We can all chip in $10 and whoever guesses the murderer wins the pot."

"Please," she said in a sarcastic drawl. "You don't even play the lottery."

Emmie laughed.

"I said that too."

"Beth, you and I both know that I'm curious about this. I don't ever want to solve a case

unless I've been thrown into it, and I was thrown into this one."

"Fair enough. So, what do we know?"

I went over the details once again as Jazzy and Beth listened intently.

"A fake name?" Beth was intrigued.

"I was just about to do a search."

Emmie had slipped away and brought her laptop into the room

"That name brings up a ton of pages," she said.

I got up and walked over to her. She sat on the couch, and I stood behind her, leaning in

to read over her shoulder. There was a podiatrist in Milwaukee; a veterinarian in Boca Raton, Florida, a mentalist in Albuquerque; a taxidermist in Montana.

"Keep scrolling," I said.

She did, but nothing interesting showed up. "James Mitchell" was too common of a

name.

"Well, that was a bust," Emmie declared before closing the computer. "Is all the ice cream gone?"

"We ate it all," Beth said. "I think I might have to call in sick tomorrow."

I laughed.

"Sorry, but I already told Emmie I was calling in sick. Besides you brought this on yourself, Beth," I said as I threw a pillow at her.

"I'll have to spend a week in the gym to get that off."

I noticed Jazzy sitting in a chair quietly watching us. That was so unlike Jazzy.

"Okay, Jazzy, spill it. What's going on?" I asked.

"The three of y'all are such good friends. I've always wanted that."

Without missing a beat, the three of us jumped up and said "Group hug" in unison, and then we rushed Jazzy with a hug. We all acted like a bunch of little girls, giggling from the sugar rush we just encountered.

"Is that all, Jazzy?" Emmie asked.

"Y'all are crazy," she said. "But I like y'all's kind of craziness."

"Why are you so serious tonight, Jazzy?"

"Well, I told you about those girls at school who said the things they did about Dr. McKinney."

"Yes," I said.

"I need to show you a couple of photos," she said as she pulled out her phone. "These are screenshots of posts that they took down. They may not mean anything, but don't you think we should at least tell Drew about this?"

She handed me her phone.

"There are two photos," she said.

I glanced down. The first screen shot said "Karma's a $#$%, McK," the second one said "'Bout time, Dr. McK. You deserved it," and a third simply hoped he'd rot.

I looked back at her and handed Emmie the phone for her to take a look.

"It might not mean anything, Miss Grace, but I'm a little afraid of Drew. He reminds me of" - she stopped and shook her head. "I got roughed up by a cop in Atlanta, and he kinda looked like Drew. It wasn't Drew, but same height, same hair."

Jazzy never talked about her past. I had no idea she'd felt that way.

"I'm sorry, Jazzy, I didn't know. I will tell you though that if Drew is anything, he's an honest cop. He may not be perfect, but he believes in upholding the law, and I would stake my life on his integrity."

She tried to smile.

"He did save my life," she said.

"And mine – twice."

I hugged Jazzy.

"No matter what he's said, I believe his bark his worse than his bite. He's got a good heart, Jazzy, and I know that he'll want to have this information."

"Thanks, Miss Grace. You'll be there with me?"

"Yes, ma'am."

We turned on the movie, but no one paid attention to it. Beth declared her evening over, and Jazzy left with her. I fell asleep on the couch, and Emmie fell asleep in the loveseat. I should've known that with all that had happened over the past two days, I'd have some sort of dream. While this one was simple, it jarred me.

I saw a stage, and a single spotlight pointed to the body directly in the middle of the light. A woman knelt at the edge of the spotlight's shadow. Her shoulders heaved as she cried over the body. But she wasn't crying for the victim. Who was she crying for? I could see his face. When I first looked at him, I saw the image of one person. I glanced at the woman kneeling over his body, and when I looked at him again, it was someone else completely.

She didn't say anything, but I could feel her thoughts. She felt relieved, but her sorrow wasn't gone. It was still there, and the emptiness was even more than it had been. Had she killed him out of revenge? But revenge for whom and why?

It jolted me awake. I sat up on the couch and took in several deep breaths.

"Grace, what is it?" I'd woken Emmie.

"Nothing. It's nothing."

"Oh no. It's never nothing," she said as she turned on the lamp. "Did you have another dream?"

"No. No dream. Nothing. I'm good. Let's go back to sleep. I have a shop to open in the morning."

"Grace Burke Ward, don't you dare lie to me. You're not getting away with it that easily. If you won't call Drew in the morning, I will, and I'll hand you the phone."

"What part of 'I don't ever want to see Drew Ward again,' do you not understand, Emmie?"

"This isn't about you. It isn't about Drew. It's about a murder."

"So what? I'm just the ex-wife of a cop. That doesn't mean anything. I'm not a detective. I'm not a police officer. I'm not in law enforcement."

"Yet, you have a ton of info that your ex-husband can use. Plus, Drew wants to know what you dreamed."

"He said that, but I really don't believe him. I want to avoid that man at all costs."

"You promised Jazzy who does have some information that might help his case. I'll let him know if you don't."

"Fine. I'll call him."

"Good, so what was the dream."

I laughed.

"You aren't giving up, are you, Emmie?"

"Nope. Grace. Not at all."

I relayed it to her.

"Any impressions about it, Grace?"

"Yes. She wasn't crying over the murder. She was mourning someone or something. She did it for someone else; not herself."

"Wow," she said. "That blows all of our other revenge scenarios out of the water, doesn't it?"

"Yes and no. The suspects seem to have revenge on their minds, but I don't know enough about any of these women to make a case."

"You don't have to figure it out. Drew does."

"True, but I don't want to talk to him."

"I'm not arguing with you. I'm going back to sleep. But I am holding you accountable for this. Good night."

With that, she turned off the light. I tried to go back to sleep, but I couldn't right away. If I'd been in my apartment, I would've gone to the computer or something. I replayed my last conversation with Drew in my head. At some point, I finally fell back to sleep.

6

We arrived at the shop early.

Emmie and I didn't talk about my dream or Drew anymore. She'd said her piece, but she gave me several dirty looks when she thought I should be calling Drew. I knew she wasn't going to let me out of calling him, and I had so much information that surely some of it would help him. After our meeting at the diner, I just couldn't bring myself to call him. His words kept ringing in my ears.

The newspaper had a follow up story on the murder. It really didn't give much information. It talked mainly about a vigil that would be held on campus, and it gave some additional information on the funeral. His obituary didn't shed any new light on who he was. It was bare bones about him being on the staff at Augusta Tech. There was nothing about his birthplace or where he went to school. A man with a doctoral degree had to have gone to a university. It was so sketchy. There were no relatives listed, which made me wonder about the estranged daughter. Of course, the comments about him from the Augusta Tech administration were glowing; the student response was reserved. The more I found out about him the more I wanted to know. Who was J.C. McKinney?

I hadn't seen or talked to Gemma since the murder. I should've called her to check on her, but I wanted to step away from it all. Instead, I'd gone deeper into it. There was no moving away from it.

I hadn't been in the office long when my phone began vibrating. It was Gemma. I stared at her name and number on the screen. This wasn't going away. I had to face it.

"Hi."

She cut me off.

"Grace, it's awful. So horrible!" she was frantic. "I don't know what to do. Grace, please come to my office."

She started talking so fast I had no idea what she was trying to say.

"Slow down, Gemma. What's wrong?"

"Please, I need you to come to the school now."

"Why? What's going on?"

I was delaying the inevitable.

"Please, I can't talk. Please just come."

"I'll be there as soon as I can."

Emmie was staring at me as I took the call. I took a deep breath.

"That was Gemma."

"Oh really?"

"Emmie, she sounded horrible. She sounded scared. I'm going to go to check on her to see what is happening with her."

She folded her arms against her chest and raised her eyebrows overdramatically.

"I know. I know. I need to call Drew, but I have this gut feeling that I will have so much more to tell him after I go see Gemma. I might as well wait until I see what's wrong with her."

"Sweetie, I have a suspicion that you could be right."

I knew it would take a good 20 minutes to get to her to see what the problem was, but I drove slower than usual. I took Gordon Highway for all its twists and turns until I reached Deans Bridge Road. At the stoplight of Gordon and Deans Bridge, I stared at the bank of trees which hid the crumbling remains of Regency Mall. Built in 1978, it was the place to shop from what I'd been told. My mother and grandmother loved to go shopping there. She told me about going to midnight showings of movies, and she got especially wistful when she talked about the J.B. White's Moonlight Madness sales where she got all kinds of great deals, then she'd sigh. J.B. White's had long since closed. It was bought out by a larger chain. It was one of her favorites. Now the mall was empty, and trees grew up around it, blocking the view from the road; there were barricades so no one could drive onto the property. The sound of a blaring horn behind me jolted me out of my daydream, forcing me to move closer to the moment I was dreading.

I parked in a visitor spot as close to the building as I could. A sign was posted to the door. It read "English department classes canceled today." I walked into the building and headed toward her office, which was at the end of the hallway. I could see her and Carolyn standing outside the door. Gemma rushed towards me as soon as she saw me.

"Oh Grace, I'm so glad you came."

"What's wrong?"

She didn't say anything just led me to her office. On her desk, I saw what was bothering her. There was a candelabra on the desk; it was covered with what looked like dried blood. There were no other signs of blood on the floor or desk, which led me to think that someone put this on her desk recently. There was only blood on the top of the candelabra. I wondered if someone had wiped the base to remove fingerprints.

"It's a prop from our production," she said. Her voice wavered. "I didn't realize how heavy it was."

"Did the police search your office yesterday?"

"Yes, they did."

She wrung her hands nervously. Her eyes darted around the room.

"Why didn't you call them?"

"Because you know them better than I do. This looks awful for me, doesn't it?"

I didn't know how to answer Gemma; instead I looked at

Carolyn. She stood frozen and expressionless as she fixed her eyes on the candelabra.

"Carolyn, did you see anything?" I seemed to have startled her with that question. She jumped when I asked it.

"No, Grace. I had left campus early yesterday for a doctor's appointment. I actually heard about the murder on the radio, and I walked in with Gemma this morning. We parked next to each other," she said. The whole time she spoke she never looked at me; she only stared at what we all assumed was the murder weapon.

My gaze followed hers, and I found myself staring at it too. I didn't touch it. I knew better. I could only stare. I'd been avoiding what I'd needed to do for several hours. I couldn't avoid it any longer.

"Gemma, we need to call Drew."

My voice caught in my throat. Tears welled in both of our eyes.

"Grace, will you stay here with me?" she asked.

"Yes, I will. For as long as I can."

I stared at my phone and then glanced at Gemma. I was surprised as Drew answered my call almost immediately.

"Grace, is everything okay?"

"Yes and no. I think you need to come to Gemma's office."

"I was heading over there, but thanks. I'll be there shortly."

"Drew's on the way."

While we waited for Drew, I thought about the scene from the guild meeting. I wondered what Abigail Prentiss meant when she said everyone had known what he'd done. What secrets did she have? On a whim, I pulled out my phone and the photo I took.

"Gemma, Carolyn, do either of you know this woman?"

I showed them the photo and zoomed in on Abigail's face.

"Of course, I do. She's McKinney's ex. She was over here last week and created quite a stir," said Gemma, who seemed to have forgotten the blood-stained candelabra. She had a story to tell me.

"Oh yes, I remember her. She's been here several times," Carolyn said.

"Really. What happened?" I asked.

"Apparently, they'd worked on a manuscript together during their marriage, and it was part of their messy divorce," Gemma explained. "Neither of them was supposed to publish it, according to a court order, but he'd just gotten a contract on it. She was furious. She threatened to sue him, and she said the only way he'd publish it was over her dead body. He just laughed. He said he'd changed a lot of it, and she couldn't prove anything."

"Wow."

"You aren't kidding. I could hear it all from my classroom."

"Carolyn, do you know of anything else?" I asked.

"I heard a few heated conversations between the two of them. One had to do with a young woman. I think it was a long-lost daughter. From the sounds of it, he'd never be named 'Father of the Year,'" Carolyn said.

"And neither of you mentioned this to Drew?"

"He's your husband, isn't he?" Gemma asked. "I saw the way he was concerned about you."

"Ex," I emphasized, without looking at her. The two letters caught in my throat. "Ex-husband. Anyway, he's on the way."

I glanced back at her and noticed a puzzled expression. I hadn't told her about my relationship with Drew, and she didn't know about Trevor.

"I'm sorry. From the way he acted around you a couple of days ago, I thought – "

"Let's talk about something else until he gets here. Are there security cameras?"

"No, they haven't worked in a couple of weeks," Carolyn said. "There was a glitch, and they needed to be replaced. Some virus infected the system, and no one around here seems to know what's going on."

Gemma was on the verge of tears. I could tell she was trying to fight them back. Her eyes pleaded with me to do something.

"Oh Grace, I didn't like the man. I mean, I strongly disliked him, but I didn't kill him. And I don't know where that came from," she pointed at the candelabra.

I touched Gemma on the shoulder.

"Gemma, Drew is an excellent detective – he's the best. He'll find the truth."

"Thank you for that compliment, Ms. Ward."

I took a breath before I turned around to see Drew standing in the doorway. Gemma reached out and touched my arm. Her hand was shaking.

"I think we have some evidence for you, Drew," I said, looking at Gemma in hopes she would speak up.

"I found that when I came to my office this morning," Gemma said, pointing to the candelabra.

Drew nodded as he went over to the desk to take a look.

"Didn't we look in here yesterday?" he asked Gemma.

She nodded nervously.

"Yes, it wasn't here then. I don't know where it came from. Is this what – "

She glanced at him, then she gripped my arm. Drew didn't say anything. He waited for her to finish.

"Do you think he was killed with that?"

He still didn't answer. His eyes bored holes in her. Drew never blinked in staring contests. I knew that first-hand. He was waiting for her to say something. He was waiting for her to slip up. If she was the killer, he was waiting to see what else might tumble out of her mouth. I tried to step away from her, but she gripped my arm. He raised an eyebrow at me, and then began to question her, rapid fire.

"Who else has access to your office?"

"I – I just found out a couple of days ago that the lock hasn't been working this whole year. They were going to repair it next week."

"What about these security cameras?"

Her face fell.

"They haven't been working either."

Drew didn't look happy. I saw his jaw clench. I desperately wanted to leave. Gemma's phone rang.

"Answer it," he said gruffly.

She let me go. I stood there for a few moments. Carolyn didn't say anything, but I'm sure someone would be asking her more questions too. It wasn't long before a couple of other deputies arrived. I slid out of the room as they started to get evidence. I lingered by the door for a few moments, but I was in the way. I wanted to stay there with her. I could see her talking with the deputies. Gemma looked up and saw me. She nodded as if to say she was going to be okay. I tried to slip away. I hoped no one – no, I hoped Drew – wouldn't notice, but I knew that wasn't going to happen. I tried to walk as fast as I could just to get out of the building.

"Going somewhere, Grace?" I heard Drew ask in his deep, authoritative, sometimes scary, detective voice.

I stopped and sucked in a deep breath. I wasn't ready to face him. I slowly turned. I glanced at the floor as I waited for him to walk toward me. I wasn't walking back toward him.

"Hi, Drew. I didn't think I was needed any longer," I said as I tried to put on a brave face to meet his gaze.

"You're always needed, Grace," he said as I winced. "Ms. Johnston apparently did because she called you instead of me. Why is that?"

I laughed nervously.

"You can be" - I paused while I searched for the right word. "Intimidating."

He nodded.

"I need to be intimidating to the bad guys."

I only nodded, but he intimidated more than bad guys.

"Grace, are you okay?"

I faked a smile.

"Yes, I'm just peachy."

Drew raised an eyebrow.

"I lived with you too long for you to try to tell me that and expect me to believe it."

"I need to get back to the shop. I have some wedding flower orders I need to do."

"Do you have anything else that would help this investigation?"

I took a deep breath. If he only knew! I thought about my piece of poster board in the back of my car with the lists of suspects and motives. I had taken off the two sticky notes with info on Dr. McKinney's possible nom de plume. I wasn't sure why. It might be important. And my dream came to mind, and then there was everything Jazzy told me.

"Why do you ask?"

He narrowed his eyes at me and stepped closer to me, invading my personal space.

"I can tell when you haven't slept, and I know you haven't. Usually you don't sleep if you have spent the night dreaming."

"Why now, Drew?"

His face softened as he reached out as though he was going to touch me, but he pulled his hand back.

"I can never apologize enough," he gently whispered. "Listen, I've said several times that you're a better investigator than I am despite what you told them in there just now. Thanks for that, by the way."

"You're good at what you do, Drew."

There was an awkward pause.

"The brain takes in more than people realize. Most people can't or don't remember everything except for those rare people with photographic memories. When you're asleep, your brain, Grace Ward makes some interesting connections. Your brain takes the facts of a scene and adds your perceptions, then it spits out these dreams of yours."

I stared at him. No one had ever said that to me about my dreams, and I'd never thought of them that way. It was an interesting hypothesis.

"You think that's all my dreams are, Dr. Ward? Me processing information?"

That came out a little sharper than I wanted. Lack of sleep and my lack of trust in him had done that to me. He raised an eyebrow at me.

"Look, Grace, I want your help. I need your help," he kept his voice soft. "You have that sensitive side to you and pick up on how people feel – if they are afraid or angry. I don't have that. Like my first murder case. It was our first case together. You knew she was in danger from the minute you saw her in the parking lot. You picked up on the non-verbal cues, and sometimes, I miss things. All of her cues processed through your brain and came out in your dream. I didn't listen to you. I've learned my lesson."

I folded my arms across my chest as I stared at him.

"You finally came up with that on your own, did you?"

"No, Dr. Blake and I talked."

That made more sense.

"Of course, you did. What did Trevor tell you?"

"What I just said. Some of your dreams can be chalked up to your observations mixed with your intuition. The two of them are powerful when combined, but your conscious mind won't allow that to happen. The knitting of the two takes place in your dreams."

"That sounds exactly the way Trevor would say something."

He shrugged his shoulders.

"That's because that's the way he said it to me."

"You two sure do talk a lot."

"Not a lot, but he doesn't waste a lot of words. When Trevor Blake says something, there's a lot of weight in it."

"Very true."

"Are you going to tell me your dream, Grace?"

I paused and gathered my thoughts.

"It wasn't much. I saw a stage and a spotlight. The body was in the spotlight, and there was a woman just outside its light. She was weeping. In dreams, you know things. Things that aren't spoken.

She didn't say anything. She just wept – bitterly. She wasn't weeping for the victim and she wasn't weeping for herself. It was like she was getting revenge, but it wasn't for something done to her. And killing him didn't bring the satisfaction she'd hoped for."

"A woman?"

"Yes."

He walked towards me and motioned for me to follow him. We walked down the hallway and turned a corner. When we were out of earshot, he stopped.

"Why do you think it was a woman?"

"You just asked what I'd dreamed last night. I am only telling you what I saw. It was a woman. I don't know what she looked like or how old she was. She was on her knees, and her body was slumped over. She buried her face in her hands. Her body shook as she cried."

He paused and stared at me. It made me uncomfortable when he looked at me. I glanced at the cracked, tile floor and put my hand on the painted cinderblock wall to steady myself.

"Anything else?"

"Whoever killed Dr. McKinney beat him beyond recognition so the woman who killed him was very angry."

"You're remembering more of what you saw the other day."

"I will never forget that, Drew. I'll never forget any of those faces. But I'll especially never forget what was left of his face."

"Is that all, Grace?"

I needed to tell him about the name, but I wasn't going to do that quite yet. I paused for a moment. Emmie was probably right when she accused me of putting that list of suspects together so I could give it to Drew. Deep down I did want to solve the case. I just didn't want to see Drew in the process. He waited for me as though he knew I had something else I wasn't sharing with him.

"What aren't you telling me, Grace? I know there's more."

"Fine," I said. "Follow me."

"What are you up to, Grace?"

"Just follow me, Drew."

I led him back to my car and pulled out my poster board. It reminded me of my days when I participated in the school science fair. This poster board showed part of my process, but in this case, I didn't have a hypothesis. I had no guess as to the person who might've killed him. I just had a list of possibilities, and the killer might not even be on my list. As Drew had said, my job was to just feed him ideas to go on.

He smiled.

"Someone was busy last night."

"Knock it off, Drew," I said. "I just needed to piece things together. There were too many people, and there was too much information for me to keep it all straight, so I made this chart."

He placed it on the trunk of the car and stared at it. I told him about the Authors' Guild meeting, the ex-wife, the mysterious daughter, the play and the possibility of a second play, my other dream, Jazzy, so many things. I pointed out each person's name and why I thought what I did. The whole time he took notes. He listened to my words. He valued what I had to say. When I'd said everything, he glanced at me.

"You were going to hold this information back?" he scolded me in that deep voice.

I glared at him.

"No. I was just going to put it on your car when I left."

"Is that so, Grace?"

"It would've saved us a conversation."

"I think you probably still would've had to talk to me."

I looked away.

"I just happened to be in the right place at the right time, and Emmie thought we should

eavesdrop. It sounded like a good idea at the time."

I glanced up to see him smiling at me. His smile still did things to my heart. I quickly

turned my attention back to the poster board.

"Eavesdropping isn't always a bad thing, Grace."

"Well, eavesdropping might not be, but this probably is," I said as I pulled out the video of Amanda Prentiss.

His mouth dropped.

"You did all of this in one afternoon?"

"Yeah, and there's one more thing."

I couldn't stop thinking about that name I'd overheard. James Mitchell. The words of that man at the Author's Guild meeting kept rolling over in my head. He said there were books in the name of James Mitchell in Dr. McKinney's office. I wanted to go into that office to see if what he said was true.

"What else are you holding back?"

I hesitated.

"Would you let me go into Dr. McKinney's office?"

He furrowed his brow. I knew that look. He was trying to decide whether to let me see it

or not.

"Hunch?" I offered. "You just asked me what I was holding back. It might be nothing, or

it could be everything."

He raised an eyebrow at that statement. I was sure the office was still part of the investigation, but they didn't know what they were looking for. They didn't know he possibly had a nom de plume although I wondered if that even mattered. I stared at Drew.

"Something in one of those conversations I eavesdropped on yesterday makes me want to look in his office. I think there may be something there that you might've missed because you didn't know what to look for."

"Come on," he said as he turned to walk back toward the building. "I'm going to put this into my car."

I followed him to his car which was only a few over from mine and then we went back to the building. I wasn't sure where Dr. McKinney's office was, but Drew knew. There was a piece of yellow police tape across the door. He broke through it. He stood back and motioned for me to go in. The last time I'd been in a college

professor's office I was a few weeks from graduation and planning
a wedding - mine. Not sure why the little things still triggered the
oddest memories connected to Drew.

All four walls of Dr. McKinney's office were bookshelves from
ceiling to floor, and they were jammed with books. I couldn't make a
rough estimate of how many were on the shelves. He was definitely
an enigma. Something didn't sit well with me on the pen name. I had
this feeling there was more to it than that.

"When we were at the Author's Guild meeting yesterday, I
overheard one of them say that Dr. McKinney had another name –
James Mitchell. I know authors do that. But he said Dr. McKinney
acted flustered when confronted with it. You know I've been
researching him. He had the air of a professor from a private four-year
college, not a two-year, state-run technical school."

Drew didn't interrupt. He listened with the same attention
Trevor always gave me.

"What if this name wasn't simply a pen name? What if there's
something he's hiding from his past, Drew?"

I walked over to his vast bookshelf. Would he have kept his
books there? I ran my eyes across the shelves, reading the spines,
searching for the pen name. As I did, I noticed classic titles   There
were books of plays and sonnets by Shakespeare, collections of
poems by Emily Dickinson and Walt Whitman. He had so many
old volumes. He had several copies of the "Strange Case of Dr. Jekyll
and Mr. Hyde." Most of the other books had only one copy. He had
multiple textbooks related to human psychology. I saw several books
on criminology. I surveyed the shelves. And yet, in the middle of the
shelves were other books about the Romantic poets. I truly believed
there was something more to all of this than met the eye. Then, I
saw the book he'd written with his ex-wife about F. Scott and Zelda
Fitzgerald. I reached for it, but Drew touched my hand before I
touched the book. I quickly moved my hand from his. He put on a
pair of plastic gloves, and he pulled the book out. In the hole it left, I
noticed something wedged in the back of the shelf.

"Drew, look behind there," I said and pointed at it.

He reached into the space and pulled out a piece of cardboard. Behind it, there were two thin volumes. On them were the pen name "James Mitchell." Drew stared at them.

"Can you tell what the books are about, Drew?"

Drew started thumbing through the pages.

"They're poems, Grace, and you know how good I am at that," he said.

"Well I know someone who might be able to help."

"It can't be Ms. Johnston."

"That part I know. I met someone at the guild meeting who might help. Her name is Lucinda Clark. She's part of the Poetry Matters group. Maybe we could analyze his style. She might be able to compare and contrast to see if it's the same person."

"Then we need to see if there's anything published under the McKinney name to compare it to."

I continued to scour the shelves. Nothing seemed to jump out. Maybe I was looking at it wrong. I was drawn to one section of a shelf. At first, I wasn't sure why. The titles were what I would've expected on an English professor's shelf "A Tale of Two Cities," "The Scarlett Letter" poetry anthologies, and one book with nothing on the spine. That seemed odd plus it was wedged between several older books with frayed spines.

"Drew, what about that one?"

I pointed to it.

It was a plain black leather book. As he pulled it out, something fell on the floor. Drew reached down and picked up a photo. He showed it to me. It was of a man holding a little girl who looked to be about 3. She had brown hair and was wearing a red and white polka-dotted dress. His gaze was fixed on her. On the back was written, "J.C. and Becca." I wondered if that was the daughter I'd heard about.

I looked over Drew's shoulder as he opened the book. On the first page was written in calligraphy "The Musings of a

Classic Wanderer: Poetry by J.C. McKinney." The poems were also handwritten. I hadn't found any poetry under his name online. Had this ever been published elsewhere, or was it his own private diary? Drew flipped through the pages. One of the poems was titled "Apology," and another "Becca Bee." I wanted to read the poems. I wondered what they were about.

"That's it, Grace. You're a natural for this. Do you have any contact information for Ms. Clark? I'll see if she can help."

"I have her card in my car, I think. Drew, do you think this is important? I feel like I'm sending you down a rabbit trail."

"I have to follow every lead I get even if it leads down a rabbit trail."

I hesitated in asking my next question.

"Drew," I started. "Never mind."

"What, Grace?"

"If you find out anything with all of this, would you let me know?"

"Yes, I will."

As we walked down the hallway, I glanced at Drew.

"Could I check on Gemma?"

"Not a good idea. They are still asking her questions."

"I feel like I'm abandoning her."

"She'll be okay. We'll run some tests on that candelabra. The autopsy results haven't been released yet. We're not ready to arrest anyone."

For the second time, he followed me to the car, and I gave him Ms. Clark's card.

"Is there anything else?"

"Jazzy. I forgot all about Jazzy."

"What do you mean?"

"She has some additional information that may or may not be useful."

"I'll follow all the leads, Grace. I want to make sure we put the right person behind bars. I'll meet you at your shop."

"Drew, remember what I told you about you being intimidating? Jazzy's not the bad guy, but you make her nervous anyway. Go easy on her, okay?"

"Yes, ma'am."

I texted Jazzy to warn her that Drew was coming to talk to her, but that I'd be there too.

He followed me to the shop, so we arrived at the same time.

"Good afternoon, ladies," Drew said as he entered the shop.

I guess it was afternoon. I'd lost track of time once again. Jazzy seemed on edge. Beth had a doctor's appointment, so she was out for the afternoon. Emmie stood in the corner of the room with her arms folded, staring at me and Drew. Jazzy had her phone ready. She told me she would try to get him out of the shop as quickly as she could. She zoomed through her screenshots.

"Mind if I hold that, Jazzy?" he asked.

"No, go ahead," she said, handing it to him.

Drew looked at one of the profiles and glanced at me.

"What's wrong, Drew?"

He turned the phone for me to see it. The name of the young woman who had posted she hoped he'd rot was Rebecca Bekah. Obviously, that was not her real name. I stared at the profile photo. All we had on that other photo was the name Becca, and there had to be millions of women named Rebecca.

"Do you think?"

"Grace, I follow every lead; no matter how slim, but you know I don't believe in coincidences."

Emmie had walked closer. She was curious now. Jazzy's eyes were big as she stared at Drew.

"Does this mean I did the right thing?" Jazzy asked.

"Yes, Jazzy, this could be important. I need to find her now," he replied. "Did you hear anyone else say anything about him? And did Rebecca say anything?"

"People called her 'Becca.' She never said he tried to do anything to her or wanted her to do stuff for grades, but she didn't like him. When other people talked about him, she always had this look on her face like she hated him. He didn't have the biggest fan club, so I just thought she was with everybody else," she said.

"Thanks, Jazzy."

"Has anyone else said anything like this to you about him?" Jazzy asked.

"From what I can tell, Jazzy, you're right about one thing. He didn't have the biggest fan club," he said, not giving away anything else in his investigation. He handed Jazzy her phone back and glanced at me. "Thank you again, Grace. And I promise to let you know something. With the information you gave me, I'm going to be pretty busy over the next few days."

I gave a simple nod in return, and I watched him leave. I wasn't really thinking about him. I was thinking more about our conversations and the books we found.

"Grace," Emmie interrupted my thoughts. "Who was that?"

I didn't answer as she continued.

"I mean he looks like Drew Ward, and he sounds like Drew Ward. But he's very different from the Drew Ward of a few months ago."

"I know. It's hard for me."

She gave me the obligatory best friend hug. I pulled away and tried to focus on something else.

"I gave him everything we had, and we found some books in Dr. McKinney's office."

"He let you in there?"

"He did. Can you believe it?" I tried to lighten things up a bit. "He didn't know what to look for, so I looked for him. We found poetry books in both names. They were hidden in plain sight, but they were there. He's going to take them to Ms. Clark to see if she thinks the two authors are the same. A photo fell out of one of those books. It was of him and a little girl. On the back, it said 'Becca.' Jazzy, can I see your phone?"

"Of course, Miss Grace."

I stared at the cryptic status for a few moments then headed to my office. I needed to do some more research.

I found her profile and noticed there was little on it. It looked like it was recently made with an obviously fake name. I wondered what her last name was. There were few photos and no information about where she was from or where she went to high school or where she lived. I wondered how old she was. Augusta Tech had students of all different ages and walks of life, so she didn't have to be right out of high school.

I needed to see Gemma. I rushed out of my office.

"Grace, where are you going?" Emmie followed me as I passed through the workroom to the back door.

"You know I've got a lead to follow."

"Grace."

"Come on, Emmie. You know I can't sit back and watch him solve this without me."

She grinned.

"Yes, you're definitely back, sweetie."

I drove faster than usual on this trek to Augusta Tech. I didn't want to miss Gemma, but I didn't want to call either.

As I went into the building, I saw Carolyn in her office.

I peered into the doorway.

"Hi, Carolyn. How did things go with the police?"

"Ms. Johnston is a wreck."

"I'm sure. How are you doing?"

"Me? I'm fine. I'm not their prime suspect. But I will tell you that Dr. McKinney's ex showed up a few other times just as I was leaving. They might've been divorced, but she still had strong romantic feelings for him."

"Really? I thought they hated each other from what you said earlier."

"I saw him kissing her one time before he closed his office door. Of course, that was before she accused him of stealing the manuscript."

I had taken a couple of Becca's photos from her profile. She had long dark hair similar to his hair color, but I'm sure that could be said of a lot of people.

"Have you ever seen this student?"

I showed her one of the photos. Carolyn tilted her head and furrowed her brow as she took her time answering the question,

"Lovely face. I think she's Ms. Johnston's student. She just started at the beginning of the calendar year."

"Really? Is Gemma still here?"

"Yes, she's finishing up a class."

"Do you remember anything about her?"

She paused.

"Not really. She met with Ms. Johnston a couple of weeks ago. I think she was going to be in that play she's doing. Why?"

"Just curious."

"Ah, I see. Is your husband going to show up again?"

I smiled.

"I would say that's a good possibility. Thanks for your help. When do you want to talk about camellias again?"

She'd seemed tense when I came in. I guess it was understandable with all that was happening, but when I mentioned the camellias, she relaxed and gave me a warm smile.

"Oh yes, I have a couple of bushes in my yard, but I'd love more," she said.

"I had some photos of my mother's camellias. I think I deleted them from my phone, but I have them somewhere else. I just need to find them."

"I'm looking forward to it," she said.

"I'll see you soon."

I headed down the hallway to Gemma's office. Her door was open, and I saw her sitting at her desk. She gave me a weak smile.

"I'm glad you came back," she said.

"I wasn't totally trying to abandon you."

"I could see you trying to get away from your ex. What happened to the two of you? I have seen the way he looks at you."

"It's complicated and convoluted and still painful, and I'd rather not talk about it to be honest."

She gave me one of those types of smiles that was meant to console someone.

"I don't understand, but I accept that. What brings you back?"

I never put the phone away, so I showed her a screenshot of the profile. Her name was visible.

"Rebecca?" she asked. She seemed confused.

"That's what her profile name is, and Jazzy told me that people called her Becca."

"Well, the name on the roll is Madison Parker."

"Any initial?"

"No, none, why?"

"Curious."

"Grace, you drove all the way out here to show me a picture because you were curious?"

I looked away. I knew she was the prime suspect. I could ruin this.

"She posted something about Dr. McKinney on social media."

"Grace, what was it?"

I showed her the other photo of the status.

"Ah, but I don't really understand because she's started during the winter quarter. She'd only been in the school for a few months, and I was her English instructor. She didn't have him. How would she even know him?"

I smiled. I'd said too much.

"I can't really answer that, but do you know anything else about her?"

"I know she's a mom. She has a wedding band so I would assume she's married. Her baby is about a year old."

"Gemma, how old is she?"

"I think she said she was 24. She's interested in a cosmetology degree."

Gemma paused and narrowed her eyes at me. She took a deep breath.

"She wrote the strangest essay a couple of weeks ago."

"How strange?"

"Well, in one of the books we read, the main character had problems with his father and a lot of anger issues. She talked about how she could relate and mentioned her hatred of her father for abandoning her," Gemma's mouth dropped, and she shook her head. "Do you think that she was McKinney's daughter?"

I shrugged my shoulders.

"I don't know the answer to that. Do you have a copy of her essay?"

"Oh yes. They email them to me, and I keep them through the end of the semester; sometimes longer."

"I think I might need to call Drew again."

Gemma hugged me.

"Thank you, Grace."

"Don't thank me yet. It may be nothing at all."

Drew didn't answer his phone when I called, which is just as well. I'd had enough interaction with him for the day. I left him a message about my conversation with Gemma and told him she might have more evidence. I also gave him the name of the student.

"I guess my police work is done for the day. I'll talk to you soon, Gemma."

"Thank you again, Grace. I'm not sure what's going to happen with the play right now and our gala. I think I'm still the prime murder suspect. Everything is up in the air. I'll have to let you know."

7

Almost a week passed with no news. I kept watching the newspaper and TV reports. There was nothing on social media. The news had begun to shift because the golf tournament would be back in town soon.

Gemma was still trying to move forward with her bid for the theater program, but she was running into resistance from the college because of the looming investigation. Although she hadn't been arrested, the deck seemed stacked against her. Several of her students had dropped out of the play including one of the lead actors.

My golf week orders had been arriving. It looked to be a busy week ahead. I was grateful to have another set of hands this year. It was hard to believe all that had happened in just a short period of time. Never in a million years would I have guessed what the year would hold. If anyone had said I'd be divorced and living over my brother's garage with a former prostitute as one of my employees, I would've laughed in their face. I never thought this was where I'd be, but it was.

I started arriving at the shop earlier so I could plan for the orders. I always needed extra flowers during the week. My friend from Charleston was planning on returning this year, and she'd put her orders in early.

I was preparing a large wholesale flower order when I heard a knock on the door. I turned to see Emmie and Beth. They flanked the door post with their hands on their hips. I knew I was in trouble. They were ganging up on me.

"You've been burning the midnight, dawn, and noon oil, sweetie," Emmie started.

"You need a break," Beth finished.

"Thanks, but I have a lot I need to do. Masters is almost upon us, and – "

"And nothing," Emmie said. "It's only 7 o'clock in the morning, and how long have you been here already?"

"I'm fine. I am the boss - remember?"

"Yes, but you're also our friend," Beth reminded me softly.

"I don't get it. I lock myself in my house for a week at Christmas and everyone thinks I'm in need of an intervention. Now that I'm out of the house and working, you still think I need an intervention. I can't win for losing with you two."

"Grace, sweetie, we love you, and you haven't stopped since then," Emmie said. "And this murder is only making things worse."

"Besides, we happen to know this really cute doctor with a great bedside manner, who is off today." Beth hinted with a big grin.

"Oh really?"

"Yes, they do, and yes, he is. And yes, he wants to spend the day with you," Trevor walked up behind them and smiled at me.

I knew he was off. I'd talked to him the night before even though I didn't see him. I stayed at the shop until after 9. Tax Day was right around the corner, and I'd fallen behind on a few things in the past couple of months. The business taxes were fine, but my personal ones still included Drew. It was complicated with the divorce. I didn't want to face it.

"I need to finish this flower order, or we won't have enough flowers for Masters Week. That can't happen."

Emmie rolled her eyes at me and turned away. Beth followed her, leaving only Trevor.

"I haven't seen you much since the English professor was killed."

"I know, and I'm sorry about that."

"Take part of the day off? It's beautiful outside. We could go to the canal and kayak, or we could walk and have a picnic."

"It's not that it's not tempting."

"Then, let me tempt you, Grace," he said and winked at me.

"I'm not going to win, am I?"

The answer to that question was a resounding "no" from two female voices.

Trevor shrugged his shoulders.

"Don't even play innocent with me, Trevor Blake. I know you are part of this conspiracy."

"Me?" he feigned innocence. "I would never"–

I held up one hand.

"No, like I said, don't go there. You're a co-conspirator. Those two don't have altruistic reasons for shooing me out of the shop."

"They are your friends, and they are concerned about you. So am I."

"How about a compromise?"

"And what would that be?"

"Let me finish this order and organize a few things. I need to go home, and you can pick me up from there around 11:30."

"Deal," the two female voices chimed in.

Beth peeked around the door.

"Your shop never closed or went into the red when I was in charge. We can do this on our own. I'll give you time to do that order, but we can handle everything else. The weddings for this weekend are already planned and we know what's coming. Besides, the busy season is coming soon enough. You need a break," Beth said.

She turned to Trevor, and I watched her wink at him.

"I'll see you at 11:30, Grace," Trevor said as he turned and walked out of the office. "Wear something comfortable."

Beth stood at the door as Emmie came back into the office.

"Sweetie, this is for your own good. You need time away from this place."

"Seriously, you just need to make up your mind, and let me finish this order. I'll leave instructions for you."

"Yes, ma'am," Emmie gave me a mock salute.

I just shook my head at both of them and turned my eyes back to my computer screen. I was tired. I hadn't been sleeping. I'd been searching the internet every night for any tidbit I could find related to Dr. McKinney and anyone on my list of suspects. There might be a lot of information on the web, but you couldn't find everything. I knew I could use a distraction. With my flower order sent, I headed back to Chateau De Burke, where I took a long shower. Well, it was as long as the hot water allowed. I still had about an hour before Trevor said he'd arrive. I'd run out of key words to search, but I thought I'd sit down with my laptop to try more phrases.

Not long after I'd nestled into a comfortable spot, I heard someone knocking on the door.

"Trevor, you're" - I didn't finished the sentence. It wasn't Trevor standing at my door. It was Drew.

"I'm not Trevor," he said.

"I can see that."

I stood with the door open, but I wasn't sure I wanted to let him in.

"I tried calling you several times, and I texted. I stopped by the shop to see if you were there. Emmie and Beth don't like me very much, do they?"

"Do you really have to ask that, Drew?" I shrugged my shoulders as he slowly shook his head.

"I guess not."

"I was in the shower. It takes forever to take a shower in there with that awful water pressure, but I guess you knew that. I wasn't paying attention to my phone, so I didn't realize you'd called."

"You're taking a day off in the middle of the week?" he raised an eyebrow. He knew it wasn't my usual thing. I'd worked six days a week for a long time except for that stint at Christmas and the few days we'd taken off the previous summer.

"It's not like Beth and Emmie gave me much of a choice. I think they fired me for the day."

I tried to laugh.

"They care about you. I know that from the reception I got at the shop."

"Oh please, Drew, you know the two of them aren't completely selfless. They have ulterior motives, believe me."

He laughed.

"Listen, Grace, I promised I'd let you know if anything came from the information you gave me. That's the reason I'm here. Can I come in?"

I hesitated for a moment.

"I'm sorry."

"No need to be," he said. "I'll put my gun on the counter and out of reach if it would make you feel better."

"No, I don't need to see your gun. You're being ridiculous. I'm not afraid of you."

"You sure about that, Grace?"

"Yes. That's not why I hesitated. I just wasn't expecting anyone, especially not you."

His gaze met mine briefly. My mind drifted back to the last time I was completely alone with him, not in a public place.

"I would've come to your shop, and I thought you'd be interested. I can leave if you want," he said softly.

"No, stop standing at my door and come in."

He smiled and came in.

"I like what you've done with the place," he said.

I didn't respond to that.

"Would you like something to drink?" I walked over to my refrigerator. "I think I have some bottled water. I don't think I have anything else."

"Thank you, Grace, but you don't have to play Southern hostess with me."

"Fine, but do you want something to drink?"

He smiled at me.

"Water is fine."

I grabbed a couple of bottles of water before heading to the small table to sit down with Drew.

"So, you have news?"

He had a huge grin on his face. I didn't quite understand that since we were talking about a murder investigation.

"You, Grace Ward, may have cracked a 30-year-old cold case."

"Really?"

"Yeah. I don't know how or if it ties into his murder, but it's a fascinating case. I believe Dr. J.C. McKinney was James Mitchell, not a pen name. That was probably his real name. I took those poetry samples to Lucinda Clark, and she believes they were written by the same person. There were similarities. She did say that you could see the maturation process of the author."

"Okay?"

"I'll tell you what I know. I ran both names, looking for any missing persons or other cases that might come up. I came across a strange cold case. The detective who'd worked on the case has been retired for a couple of years, but he remembered it well. James Mitchell was a person of interest in the death of Thomas Matthew McKinley. McKinley and Mitchell went to school together in Texas. They were college roommates. McKinley was from an upper middle-class family near New Orleans, and Mitchell was from a blue-collar family near Chicago."

I took a sip of water and listened to Drew tell the story.

"They seemed to get along. They both pledged a fraternity and were accepted. At this school, freshmen were not allowed to live in the fraternity house, so they remained in the dorms they were assigned. Thomas invited James to spend the summer at his family's home. And James did. Their sophomore year, the two returned to school to live in the frat house. Members of the fraternity said that Tom and Jim, as they were known, had a striking resemblance to each other when they came back sophomore year. They had the same

123

build; the same color hair and the same haircut. Both of them wore glasses. Tom decided to ditch glasses and go for contacts, and Jim did the same. At Thanksgiving break, Jim was going to go home with Tom. There wasn't anything spectacular about the trip, but the two never returned to school."

I leaned forward as he continued to tell his story. He paused to take a sip of water.

"Tom's mother filed a missing person's report. No one ever filed a report on Jim, but no one ever reported that he returned to school either. As it turns out the whole 'blue collar family from Chicago' was a lie. Jim was from a small town in Idaho. His parents were killed by a drunk driver when he was 8. He bounced around from foster home to foster home. He ran away and ended up in the juvenile justice system in Illinois. Somehow, he got into college; he seemed to be trying to turn his life around."

"Okay, Drew, I'm completely lost."

"I'm getting there. About two months after he was reported missing, Tom's body was found in a burned-out vehicle registered to the McKinleys. They found the vehicle in Dallas, nowhere near the school or his hometown. Tom's parents discovered that the school savings account they'd opened for Tom was empty. The bank manager didn't know of Tom's disappearance, but he reported that someone who looked like Tom came to the bank after Thanksgiving break and cleaned out the account. Tom had a twin brother, John Chadwick McKinley. The brothers were born premature, and John had several birth defects. He died when he was about 18-months-old. We think that J.C. McKinney is a derivative of John Chadwick McKinley."

"Wow."

"Tom's parents are deceased. The retired detective thinks there may have been an older sibling, but he wasn't sure if it was a sister or brother. After their parents died, the sibling disappeared. He said he'd check his files for more information, but I haven't heard back yet. They used dental records to ID the body."

"So, you think Jim, James or whatever his name is took the

twin brother's identity?"

"You're good, Grace. Yes. It was easier to falsify documents back then. He was in the McKinley home and could have found the birth certificate or he could have gotten one himself."

"But the different last name?"

"Like I said, things were easier to fake. With a birth certificate, he could've come up with a whole new identity."

"This doesn't sound like I helped to solve anything, Drew. It just sounds like I opened up another can of worms."

Drew laughed.

"Yes, ma'am. This is a mess."

"Interesting rabbit trail, but does it have anything to do with who killed him?"

"That part I don't know yet. It doesn't seem to. It doesn't seem like either of them had any living relatives."

I glanced down at the table trying to connect the dots on the things I knew about him. Some of that actually made sense. He was interested in acting, and he could've just been playing a role the whole time. If he was a fugitive, that would explain why he tried to stay under the radar and didn't have much of a digital footprint.

I glanced up to see Drew staring at me.

"Wow."

He laughed.

"And all because you were eavesdropping?"

"I believe I got into some hot water with you over eavesdropping once."

He nodded.

"Touché."

He paused as though he wanted me to say something. I was still trying to digest what he'd told me.

"Do you have any other info for me, Grace?"

"Such as?"

"How much have you talked to Ms. Johnston?'

I took a deep breath.

"I've only talked to her once since that day you found the murder weapon – I guess that was the murder weapon. She called to let me know that the play, the gala everything was on hold pending the investigation. She was not happy. She cursed Dr. McKinney's name."

"Do you think she'd talk to you?"

"I wanted to check on her."

"That might be a good idea."

I didn't say anything. My mouth dropped as I stared at him.

"Wait a minute. You want me to interrogate your suspect?"

"No, that's not what I said. Don't put words into my mouth."

"You think I can get additional information out of her, don't you?"

"I can only hope."

"So where exactly is this investigation?"

"Wait mode. The crime lab takes time. Here's what I have, and I'm trusting you not to tell anyone. The ex-wife has an ironclad alibi for the day of the murder, the two students who made the accusation have recanted. I researched your author guild contacts, and I found another author, Jack Pennington, who had a beef with the victim and was seen arguing with him the day before the murder, but he also has an alibi that checks out. The main suspect seems to be Gemma Johnston, but I don't have enough to arrest her yet. Gemma's fingerprints were on that candelabra. They weren't the only ones though. There were a couple of others. I don't know who they belong to."

"It's not her," I blurted out.

Drew raised an eyebrow.

"How can you be sure?"

"Why would she? I mean, he was a condescending jerk who stole her work, but she had so many plans. Was there anyone else in his department who could've done it?"

"We interviewed everyone who worked in the department. They were either in class or at their desk doing something. Everything has a time signature on it."

"And no one saw anyone suspicious coming out of the building?"

"Grace, are you the detective, or am I?"

"Well, you're the one who keeps telling me I should change careers."

He smiled.

"All of the security cameras mysteriously seemed to have not been working that morning."

"And no one heard anything, Drew?"

"Nothing."

"I find it hard to believe."

"I like that healthy skepticism."

I folded my arms against my chest and stared at him.

"Who are you?"

"I'm trying to be a better man than I was, Grace. I want you to at least not be afraid of me. You aren't nearly as nervous right now as you were when you saw me standing on your doorstep a little bit ago."

I glanced away. He was right. I wasn't afraid. I'd fallen back into the same sense of comfort I'd always had in his presence.

"What about the estranged daughter?"

He laughed.

"Took you long enough to ask. The woman in Ms. Johnston's class is his daughter."

"Why didn't you say so, Drew? I can't believe you waited for me to ask."

"I wanted to keep you in a little suspense," he said.

"Seriously? That woman is his daughter."

"Yes, she registered under her middle and married names – Madison Parker. But you wouldn't have recognized her by her maiden name anyway. She used her mom's name, not McKinney's. When he visited Virginia for that leave of absence a few years ago, he went to visit Lacey, his ex-girlfriend, Becca's mom. Becca didn't know the reason for the visit. I don't know if they rekindled their romance, but Dr. Prentiss filed for divorce the day he returned from that trip. Lacey wouldn't tell him where his daughter was. Not long after his visit, Lacey was diagnosed with an aggressive form of ovarian cancer and died within a couple of months. On her deathbed, she told Becca about her father. Becca didn't want to just show up and meet him. She was stealthy about it. She planned it out and enrolled as a student. She wanted to watch him, to decide whether she really wanted to meet him. She considered his death a second abandonment, and she was angry at him. She never had the chance to tell him who she was. I know that's not the greatest explanation for her angry status, but that's her story. I'm still checking into it. She was in Ms. Johnston's play, and her fingerprints were also on the candelabra."

I stared at him with my mouth open. I started to ask another question when there was a knock on the door. That had to be Trevor. I looked down at my phone. I'd been talking to Drew for almost an hour. Drew stood up as I moved to open the door.

Trevor was dressed casually. He wore a pair of shorts and a T-shirt.

"Dr. Blake," Drew greeted Trevor.

The two men exchanged handshakes. Trevor's furrowed brow and intense gaze asked all sorts of unspoken questions.

"Drew was telling me that I may have helped in solving a 30-year-old cold case," I interjected.

I hoped that would answer some of Trevor's questions. He didn't look at me when I spoke though. That was unusual for him. He'd turned his attention to Drew, and now he and Drew were locked in a steely stare.

"Grace provided some incredible information on this case and the cold case. She's an amazing woman," Drew said without flinching and without breaking their gaze.

"Yes, she is amazing, Drew," Trevor said icily. I only heard that tone of voice when he talked about his father.

The two kept up the standoff for a few more moments before Drew looked at me and smiled.

"I'll be leaving now. You two enjoy your day."

He walked to the door, and I followed him.

"Thank you, Drew, for telling me everything you did."

"You're welcome, Grace. If you hear anything else about what we talked about, please let me know."

"I will."

I closed the door and waited before I turned to Trevor.

"Are you all right?" he asked.

"I'm fine. Where are we headed?"

He reached for my hand.

"Are you sure?"

"Yes, I admit being nervous when he first got here, but all he wanted to tell me about was where a piece of information I gave him led. It was interesting. How about I tell you on the drive to wherever we're going?"

"That sounds like a plan."

8

As he opened my car door, I noticed a picnic basket in the back seat.

"Should I have brought anything?" I asked as he got into the car.

"Not a thing. We're heading to the lake. My brother, James, has a house there. He said we could take the boat out if we wanted. He has a fantastic deck. We can eat on the deck or spread a blanket out under some of those tall pine trees. Whatever you want. At this time of year during the week, there won't be too many people on the water. It should be nice and relaxing."

"What happened to going to the Augusta Canal?"

"I wanted to keep you guessing," he said and winked.

He took his time driving to the lake. The lake is a popular place to go. It's a manmade lake with a dam designed for flood control and hydropower among other things. It borders both Georgia and South Carolina. The Army Corps of Engineers created the lake and dam between 1946 and 1954.

Technically, it's the J. Strom Thurmond Dam, named after U.S. Sen. Strom Thurmond from South Carolina, who served as a senator for 48 years and died in 2003 at the age of 100. The lake is also supposed to bear his name. My mother said Georgians didn't like the idea of their lake being renamed after a South Carolina senator. Most Augustans I know still call it what it was originally named -

"Clarks Hill." There is a town by that name on the South Carolina side of the lake.

When it's at full pool, the lake includes 71,000 acres of water and 1,200 miles of shoreline in several counties in both states. There are recreation areas with beaches, and many people have homes on land near the water. People camp on the lands, and it's a fisherman's paradise.

I'm not a fan of swimming in the lake. The water is murky, and parts of the shoreline are thick Georgia clay. You've never known what gross feels like until your feet have sunk into that fiery orange, slimy clay, and it oozes between your toes. Being on the water on a boat is relaxing, but Drew and I didn't go out on boats too often. We didn't own one. During the past few years, we were too busy to take time to enjoy life. Maybe that was one of our problems. He said he'd taken up fishing, so I guess he reconnected with a friend who had a small jon boat. Any time we went to the lake, we'd go to a park and enjoy a picnic.

I tried to imagine Trevor's brother and sister-in-law's place on the lake. His sister-in-law Claire was like Trevor, super neat and everything in its place. She was the type of person who could actually keep white carpets clean – with three boys. I couldn't keep carpets clean with just Drew and me. I was sure the place was beautiful. Some people lived at the lake year-round while some had a getaway place like Trevor's family. The residences ran the gamut of small log cabins to mansions and everything in between.

I finished telling Trevor my story then relaxed in the seat and listened to the radio.

"Are you hungry?"

Was I hungry? I hadn't really thought about it until he said something.

"I am."

"We can eat first and then maybe go for a walk. Or like I said we can go out on the boat. We have all day to do whatever you'd like."

I smiled. I didn't want to hurt his feelings, but what I really wanted to do was take an overly long nap.

The closer we got to the property the more the roads snaked around. There were lovely houses, - A-frames, log cabins and a few single wide mobile homes. Trevor turned into what didn't even look like a driveway. The house was underneath the beautiful towering pine trees. It was a mid-century contemporary two-story, wooden-framed house with a deck on the side.

When he opened the door, the first thing I noticed was the back of the house was glass from floor to ceiling. My mouth dropped. The windows gave a full view of the beautiful, calm lake and the soaring trees against the backdrop of the cerulean sky.

"This is beautiful," I passed Trevor and walked straight to the windows to stare.

"I had a feeling you'd like it."

I turned back to him.

"If this was my house, I don't think I'd ever want to leave it."

"James and Claire used to come up here a lot when the boys were little, but as time passed, soccer tournaments became the order of business on the weekend. The lake house isn't used quite as much now. Just for a few days in the summer."

I glanced around. Everything was in Claire's signature white. The large great room had a beach theme; the walls were a white bead board; the couches were overstuffed with white pillows except for strategically placed, bright turquoise accent pillows. Shells sat atop the coffee table, and beach scenes adorned the walls.

"There's a bedroom through that door," said Trevor as he gave me an impromptu tour. "There's another bedroom and bath upstairs. And you walked through the kitchen."

I walked back to the windows.

"Would you like to walk to the dock, or would you like to eat on the deck? It has a great view too."

"Let's eat on the deck and then walk to the water."

He headed to the deck on the side of the house, climbed its stairs, and placed a blanket over the dusting of yellow pollen. Spring had indeed sprung in the area. Once again, I was grateful I was not allergic to the pine pollen. As he readied the spot, I stared into the distance. He was right. From the higher vantage point, the view was even more incredible outside than it was inside. The pines shaded the deck making it a wonderful spot to enjoy the sounds of the birds in the trees. In the distance, I could hear a woodpecker chiseling into a tree in search of its next meal.

"Grace, lunch is served."

I turned to see the contents of the picnic basket neatly aligned on the blanket. There were small plates and wine glasses with a bottle of sparkling grape juice, cheese, grapes and strawberries. He'd made turkey wraps with spinach tortillas, tomato and lettuce. There was hummus and crackers.

"You think of everything."

"I try. I may have a couple of chocolate chip cookies somewhere," he said and winked at me.

"Where?"

"That's my secret for now," he said. "Did Drew's visit upset you?"

"Not terribly until the death stare between the two of you. I wasn't sure what was going to happen with that."

"He and I have an understanding."

"I couldn't tell by that standoff."

"I'm sorry, Grace. I didn't mean to upset you."

Something was bothering him, and it wasn't Drew. I hadn't realized it until now.

"You were awfully quiet on the ride up here, Trevor."

He smiled.

"You were telling me about Drew's investigation. It was quite interesting, even if it was a rabbit trail."

"What's the matter?"

He seemed surprised and didn't answer the question, so I pressed him.

"You never let me get out of telling you what's on my mind.

Now, Trevor, it's your turn to tell me."

"I've enjoyed being part of the clinic. It was never designed to be a permanent job. You know I went there on a temporary basis until they filled the position," he said.

I nodded.

"I've been seeing one patient. He's a diabetic, but he refuses to take his insulin. He died last night in the ER," he continued.

"I'm sorry, Trevor."

"It was completely avoidable, but he refused to take the medication. Losing patients is hard, even though I've only been there a few weeks, I'd seen that gentleman several times."

"Is that the only thing on your mind?"

He took a breath.

"Remember when I told you that a professor at the medical college might be retiring?"

"Yes."

"Well, it's official now. All three of my brothers admired him. And all three of them ganged up on me this week to get me to consider applying for the position. The college is doing a search now."

I smiled as I tried to picture him in a classroom.

"There would be classroom as well as some hospital work, but the hours would be regular ones. I wouldn't be fighting with insurance companies over treatments. I'd still be interacting with people," he paused and tilted his head. "Why do you keep smiling like that?"

"I'm just imagining all of those medical students wanting to sign up for Dr. Blake's class. If I knew you were going to be my professor, I'd take every class you were teaching."

"Is that so?" he smiled and tilted his head at me.

"Absolutely!"

"Thank you for your vote of confidence, I think. It's not a given. I might not even get an interview."

"Are you going to apply for it?"

"My CV is up-to-date. Do you have an opinion?"

I felt my mouth drop as he asked that, and I stared at him for a moment.

"Did I say something wrong, Grace?"

"No, I'm just surprised that you want my opinion."

"Why wouldn't I want your input? My brothers freely gave me theirs; obviously, they don't like my decision to leave the practice in North Carolina. They've ever so politely introduced me to several oncologists in hopes of me joining a practice here. They don't mind having me back in town. But now that most of our parents' estate has been settled or is well on the way to being settled, they think I 'need to accomplish something with my life.' Those were their words. They are trying to save face by having me at least do something they deem useful."

"What do you want, Trevor?"

He smiled.

"Besides wanting people to stop telling me how to live my life?"

"Yes."

"I want to help people. I want to do something that matters. Yes, I love to cook, but I don't want to own or work at a restaurant – although I've considered it just to spite my brothers," he said and winked. "But that's another career that consumes your time. I want to have time. I want to have a life."

He paused and looked into my eyes as he continued.

"I want to have a life with you," he said.

I smiled. There was something about the way he said it that made my heart melt.

"Have you ever wanted to teach?"

"Actually, I have. I've dealt with med students before. I enjoyed the interaction, and I'd still get some patient interaction too."

"So, you didn't really hate medicine?"

"I told you I enjoyed parts of it. It wasn't my choice to go into that field."

"What would've been your choice?"

"Honestly, I used to think about being a high school music teacher or maybe a math teacher and being the coach of the cross-country team."

I smiled.

"I think you know what you should do, then, Trevor."

"I think so. Thank you, Grace."

"What for?"

"For being there. For listening to me and hearing me. You're the only one who has ever really done that in my life. Everyone else always wanted to tell me what to do."

Lunch was light but filling. We ate the rest of our meal in silence. My eyes kept being drawn back to the water though. I couldn't help it. I loved being around water. It had been so long since I'd been on a boat, and I could feel the water calling to me.

"You keep staring at that lake. Am I going to have to take you on a boat ride?"

"I'd love that."

"Come on then," he said as we gathered the remains of the lunch.

It was a short walk to where the boat was docked.

"Does James leave the boat here all the time?" I asked as he helped me in. He sat down next to me on the white seats of the speedboat.

"No, but when I asked him about borrowing his house for the afternoon, James said he'd throw in the boat too if I'd ride up here with him to put it in the water. While you were working on Saturday, we drove up and went out on the water for a while. My oldest brother, Richard, decided to join us and he took advantage of the fact that I was a captive audience for a couple of hours. That's how I found out that Richard, thinks I'm 'throwing my life away,' and that I 'needed to take my medical degree seriously.' I believe he even told me I needed to grow up."

"Wow, that's harsh."

"He sounded just like my dad," he said as his jaw tightened.

"Richard has always been the worst; I guess it has to do with him being the firstborn. James isn't as bad, but he wants me to stay in the medical profession. He follows the family line on that one. James doesn't pressure me as much usually, but Richard has the stronger personality of the two of them."

"Trevor, I'm sorry. You didn't" -

"What?"

"We didn't need to" -

"I didn't need to take you away from everything for a while. Is that what you wanted to say?" he asked. "When was the last time you even went outside of Augusta's city limits?"

"Drew took me to Edisto last June. We stayed at Beth's beach house for several days. It was wonderful."

"And what's happened since June?"

"A lot."

"Exactly. Besides, I can handle my brother, correction, my brothers. Like I said, James isn't as bad. I'd prefer to stay away from Richard at all costs."

"He doesn't like me much, does he?"

Trevor looked at me and paused before saying anything.

"Richard doesn't like anyone."

I took a breath. That meant "no."

"Trevor, I would support you in any occupation you chose. That's what friends are for."

He responded by handing me the cloth beach bag he'd been carrying. I opened it to see sunscreen. I smiled.

"I don't need to lecture you about the dangers of the sun; do I, Grace?"

"No, I burn with sunscreen on, which is the reason I never was a sun worshipper."

"Good. Less chance of skin cancer."

He fired up the boat, and we slowly headed out of the cove. Once in open waters, he sped up. I couldn't hear anything over the engine's roar. Trevor was usually even-tempered, but our conversation about his three older brothers had upset him. He was going a little faster than I would've liked, but I just held on for the ride. I tried to take in the scenery. The weather was gorgeous. The temperatures were in the 70s, and the sky was slightly overcast.

We'd been out on the water for about 45 minutes when Trevor slowly brought the boat to a stop. He turned off the motor and came to sit next to me again. The waves lapped against the side of the boat gently rocking it. In the distance, I could hear the screeching of a hawk. With no other boats on the water, it was peaceful.

"Do you want to jump in?" Trevor asked and winked at me.

"No, don't, Trevor." I panicked when I said that.

He seemed surprised as he sat down next to me.

"What's the matter?"

I tried not to be afraid. It reminded me of my dreams of Drew drowning. I knew those were only figurative dreams; they represented him drowning in his emotions. I tried to play it off.

"For starters, the water is too cold, and I can't see what's under the surface. There's no way I'm jumping in that."

He laughed.

"Have you ever been to the Caribbean?"

"No."

"You'd love it. Powder sand beaches and turquoise waters. You can see what's under the surface there."

"Sounds like heaven."

He smiled and started to say something, but he shook his head instead. I had a feeling I knew what he was going to say. I would've been willing to bet it had something to do with it being a great place for a honeymoon or that he'd like to take me there some day.

"Are you having a good time?" he asked instead.

"Yes. You're one person who can kidnap me anytime."

He reached out for my hand and held it. Neither of us said anything else. I lost track of time and of everything else as we sat there. I watched as a flock of Canadian geese flew overhead in

ormation. We saw a few fish jumping out of the water. Finally, he
started the boat again. We stayed on the water for about an hour
before we pulled back into the quiet cove. He guided me into helping
him moor the boat.

"You were starting to turn a little pink," he said as we walked
back to the house.

"Like I said, I burn easily."

"I remember one summer when you were as red as a lobster."

"Me too. And that happens when I'm not even trying to get
sun."

Once back inside, I sat down on the white-cushioned couch.
It seemed to swallow me.

"When we came up the other day, I also brought food so I
could cook for us."

I got up and followed him into the kitchen. It was a galley
kitchen with barely enough room for one person let alone two. He
stood at the doorway into the tiny kitchen and barred me from
coming in.

"I'll handle this. You go and rest."

"I'm fine. You don't need to do this."

"Go! Doctor's orders."

"Yes, sir."

The house was equipped with a surround-sound stereo, and
he turned the music to some smooth jazz. I let the soft couch and its
multitude of pillows envelope me. It wasn't long before I'd drifted off
to sleep. It was no secret that I dreamed a lot. But since I'd begun to
witness so much death and evil, my dreams had gotten darker. I saw
the victims' faces. I even saw Jillian's face after Drew shot her. There
were other dreams too. The first murder victim was the hardest. I'd
see her in my dreams face up in the Savannah River entangled in the
vines. She was so young. In my dreams, she'd sometimes get up and
walk on the water. She'd climb over the green railing on the Riverwalk
and stagger toward me with the vines dragging behind her.

"Why didn't you save me?" she'd ask. "I know you saw me. I

know you knew I was afraid. I tried to signal you to help. I know you could've done something. Why didn't you help me?"

She kept saying it over and over as she came closer to me. All I did was back away from her. At one point, I couldn't go back any further, and we were eye-to-eye.

I'd had that dream several times. I'd told no one. I didn't write it in my book. Every time I'd had it, I woke up sobbing, gasping for air, and drenched in sweat.

I could feel pressure on my arms. I could hear someone calling my name. I couldn't wake up. In my dream, I screamed at her to forgive me. I broke down in tears in front of her and fell to the ground, pleading with her. It was at that point that I heard my name again. I opened my eyes. I could see Trevor, but in the moment that I woke up, I didn't know who he was. I didn't know where I was or what day it was.

"Grace."

As he said my name again, I realized who he was, and I saw the look of sheer horror in his eyes. I was lying on the couch, and he was seated on the edge next to me; he had one hand on each arm. He moved as I sat up. I knew he wanted me to say something. I wondered what I'd done in my sleep. He cut through my thoughts.

"You were thrashing around, and saying 'no, please, no,'" he said.

I touched my face. My cheeks were wet. My throat felt scratchy. I had a feeling I wasn't saying things but screaming them instead. I turned to see him staring at me, waiting for me to say something.

"Is this what you've been trying to hide from me?" he whispered.

"Yes," I could barely utter the word.

He pulled me to his chest and leaned back on the couch, letting me cry. He didn't say anything; he stroked my hair, and I could hear him gently humming. He'd turned off the jazz. After several minutes, I pulled away from him and sat up. I tried to collect my thoughts. He'd just witnessed something I didn't want him to see. I tried not to look at him. I looked straight ahead, but I could see him out of my peripheral vision. I ran my fingers through my hair. The dream was so vivid. I could still see her after I'd awoken even though she wasn't there, and the dream wasn't real.

"The first murder case last April. I think I told you about it."

"Yes, you did."

I turned my body on the couch to see him better.

"It was a young girl involved in the human trafficking ring we got Jazzy out of. You know you have said wonderful things about how I've helped Jazzy, but I don't know if I've helped her for the right reasons."

He reached out for my hand and gripped it tightly as I continued.

"I've always been angry at Drew for not listening to me. If he'd listened to me and done something, the young woman who I found in the Savannah River, might still be alive. I think I helped Jazzy because of the guilt."

"Grace, in the case of Jazzy, it doesn't matter if that's the reason. You helped her, and that's all that matters."

I stood up and turned my back toward him.

"But I didn't save her. She was just a kid. I didn't save her."

I started to cry again. Trevor walked over to me.

"Look at me, Grace," he said.

I looked into his face.

"You can't save everyone," he whispered. "That's a harsh reality. Believe me, I know. I've tried to save people, and I couldn't. That's what makes my career choice so hard. People die even when you want them to live."

He pulled me into his arms again, and I cried even more. I wasn't sure how the tears kept coming. In my mind, I was so over all the crying, but apparently, part of me didn't get that message.

"I see her in the dream. She gets up out of the water, and she blames me for not saving her."

He pressed me close to him and kissed my temple.

"Thank you. I'm sorry, Trevor. I didn't want you to see that."

He looked hurt.

"I'm glad I did. You couldn't hide it forever. You never had this dream when you were married to Drew?"

"No, I used to dream about him drowning and calling out to me, but I couldn't save him either. I felt so guilty for our relationship ending."

"Is that the reason you got so upset when I threatened to jump in earlier?"

"Yes. I couldn't bear it if anything happened to you."

"You can't blame yourself for Drew. He's an adult. He has to take responsibility for his own actions," he said sternly. "Remember what I told you this afternoon about my patient who died because he refused to take his insulin."

"Yes."

"I couldn't save him either. I wanted to."

I took a deep breath, and Trevor stepped toward me once again. He wrapped his arm around my waist, pulling me close. He kissed my forehead.

"Please, don't push me away," he whispered into my ear. I rested my head against his shoulder. I felt safe with him. I don't know how long we stood there. I never wanted to leave. He kissed my forehead a second time and released me.

"Grace, you keep talking about saving the world, but there's one person I need you to help me save."

"Okay?" It was more of a question than statement.

"It's you. You told me you wanted to just stay friends as you tried to work through your feelings about Drew and the divorce. And I will do that. But there are some things you need to face and deal with. You have deep anger toward Drew. You are angry at him for not listening to your warning and saving the girl; you're angry at him for not saving himself; you're angry at him for leaving you; you're angry at him for putting you in danger and not protecting you."

He was right. I drew in a deep breath as he continued.

"You want to save the world, but I see someone in front of me who needs saving. And together we can do that. We can save you, but you have to want to be saved. I want to be part of your world, but every time I feel like I'm getting close, you put up another wall. Listen, I have a couple of business cards for therapists."

He paused briefly. Trevor was always determined to say the right things. He never just blurted out things like I did sometimes.

"You're always interested in doing things for others, and part of me really wants to ask you to do this for me if you won't do this for you. I can't do that though. You have to want this for yourself."

"Yes, you're right. I don't want to burden anyone."

I glanced down. He edged closer to me and tilted my chin until I couldn't help but stare into his beautiful blue eyes.

"I've said it before, and I'll say it again," he said softly. "You're never a burden to me. Don't ever forget that."

"Thank you."

"If you want to thank me, then get help for you," he said.

He paused briefly and then his concerned look melted into a mischievous grin. "I don't want to be in the friend zone forever." He winked at me.

I laughed.

"That's much better, Grace," he said.

He smiled.

"Now, I have to finish cooking."

I followed him into the tiny kitchen.

"You sure you don't need my help."

"No, I'm more than capable in the kitchen."

"You're better than I am," I laughed because it was the truth. He was much better than I was. "It smells wonderful."

"It's a chicken with a balsamic reduction and some vegetables. You'll love the dessert though. Brownies and ice cream."

I laughed.

"Emmie's starting to rub off on you."

"Simple is best; don't you think? There's a salad in the refrigerator. Why don't you put it on the table?"

As always, anything that Trevor cooked was amazing. We'd gotten into a routine with meals. He'd do the cooking, but I'd offer my help. He'd refuse. I'd clean, but when he offered to help with that, I'd let him.

We spent the rest of the evening talking about mundane things; the weddings I had scheduled for the weekend and the flower orders that were pending for the hoopla around golf tournament week.

He drove me back home and followed me upstairs to the door. We paused outside.

"Do you want to come in, Trevor?"

"No. While I'd love to, I have to be up early tomorrow, and you probably need to get some sleep. Hopefully better than the nap you tried to have."

I nodded.

"Thank you for a wonderful day, and again I'm sorry" -

He didn't let me finish that statement. Before I knew what was happening, he'd pulled me into his arms for a slow sweet kiss, taking my breath away. I couldn't remember the last time a kiss had made me feel the way that one did. I didn't want it to ever end. As cliché as it was, I felt a kaleidoscope of butterflies in the pit of my stomach.

"What were you saying, Grace?" he asked as he let me go.

I could see his face under the porch light. He smiled mischievously. What was I saying? In that second, I honestly couldn't think of anything except that kiss.

"I was saying that you have the most beautiful eyes," were the words that tumbled from my lips.

He smiled and touched my cheek

"I thought that's what I heard."

He reached into his pocket, taking out a couple of business cards and pressing them into my hand.

"Here are a couple of options. Both specialize in trauma, PTSD, and depression. If you don't like them, we'll find someone else."

He touched my cheek.

"You want to save the world, but not yourself, Grace. It doesn't work that way. Please do this – for you, for your future."

"For you?"

"I would love to say for me, Grace, but you can't do it for me. You have to do it for you and you alone. Yes, there are people who love you – your parents, your brother, Emmie, Beth and Jazzy. And me too. We all want you to take care of yourself. PTSD will take its toll. You saw what happened with Drew and how it destroyed the two of you. Don't let it win again."

I nodded.

"I'll make an appointment tomorrow, Trevor."

"Promise me."

"I promise."

"Good night, Grace," he said as he kissed me once again. This time it was brief, but it still affected me the same. I stood at the door, trying to catch my breath, and watched him leave.

9

I woke up refreshed. I don't know the last time I would've described my sleep as refreshing but the day on the lake, in the sun and in the peaceful company of an amazing man did me a world of good. I even had a dream – not a nightmare - during the night. That was surprising because dreams often jarred me from my fitful sleep. Instead it rushed through my brain the moment I woke up. In the dream, Gemma was crying. She was afraid that Drew was going to arrest her, but I told her she had nothing to worry about because I knew who'd killed Dr. McKinney, and it wasn't her. That was puzzling because I had no idea who'd killed him, but then Jazzy showed up. In her thickest Cajun drawl, she said 'Hon, you have the answer. It's been staring right at you the whole time.

It was 5:30 a.m. That was later than I'd been getting up lately. It was probably too early to call Gemma, but Drew had asked me to check on her. The dream and his urging gave me an excuse to see what was going on.

Some of what Drew had told me about that cold case lingered in my brain. I wondered if I could find anything else. I searched for the names of the McKinley family, but nothing relevant to what he'd told me popped up. It was frustrating. I sat back and stared at the screen of my laptop when someone knocked on my door. I opened it to find Zack outside.

"Good morning," I said as he shoved a paper bag and a cup

into my hand and walked in. He'd bought a chicken biscuit and some sweet tea. Heaven at this time of the day. I was surprised though because he usually left around 6 a.m. to beat traffic at Fort Gordon's gates.

"And how did you sleep last night?" he asked.

"Fine. Just fine," I said as I took a test sip of what he'd given me. It was sweet tea; my morning elixir. He didn't say anything; he just stared at me.

"What, Zack?"

"That was an awfully long kiss last night with someone who's 'just a friend,'" he said, emphasizing the phrase I said so often.

"Were you spying on me?"

"No, but I do look out the window when a car pulls up in my driveway late at night."

"It wasn't that late. I went to bed right after he left, and it wasn't even 10."

"I thought I'd try to get the news before Emmie and Beth."

"There's no news except that Drew stopped by yesterday and told me I might've helped with a cold case."

"That's pretty cool, sis, but that didn't give you the twinkle in your eyes that I see this morning."

I took a breath and tried to ignore that remark.

"I've been up this morning trying to find things on the internet about it, but it's so old, nothing pops up."

I folded my arms across my chest and stared at him for a moment.

"Thanks for breakfast, by the way, but why are you here?"

"Last night, Drew called me. Seeing you has been hard on him."

I glanced at the floor as my brother continued.

"He wanted me to be there, so he didn't turn somewhere else."

I snapped back to stare at him.

"Wait, Zack, I thought he was doing okay."

"He is but being back in this place – this apartment - brought back a lot of memories of some long conversations he and I had. Seeing you and knowing he's not over you is hard on him."

"Why are you telling me this? Pardon my lack of sympathy, but he has no one to blame but himself. He's the one who wanted the divorce not me," his statement riled me up. My words flew out of my mouth in a sharp tone.

Zack grinned smugly.

"What? I wasn't the one who filed." Then it hit me what he was doing.

He nodded.

"Exactly, Gracie. You weren't the one. It's his own fault. I'm glad you're realizing that. I'll send you my bill in the morning."

"Is that all you wanted to tell me?"

"That, and I think he might be planning to make an arrest in that case soon."

"Really? But he told me yesterday morning he was waiting for some evidence and that he wasn't going to be making any arrests any time soon. Did something change?"

Zack shrugged his shoulders.

"Something must've. Because he told me he was close. I thought you'd want to know."

"You think he's arresting Gemma?"

"It's possible. I know she's your friend."

"Thanks. I know she didn't do it though. I just don't know how to prove that."

"You'd better think fast," he said. "I've got to go."

I watched as Zack headed out the door, and I noticed the two business cards Trevor had given me lying on my table. I picked them up and read the names. One of the therapists was a man and one was a woman. I trusted Trevor's judgement in this, but I probably would feel more comfortable with a woman. I tucked them into my purse and headed to the shop.

Everything was neat and in order. Emmie had written on the

white board the orders that had come in and what had been delivered. She also had notes about the weddings coming up over the weekend. Sometimes I honestly didn't think I was needed in my own shop. I retreated into my office to work on the tax information I didn't get to finish the day before. I was close to finishing when I heard a knock on my door and turned to see Emmie standing there.

"So how was your date yesterday?" she winked as she said it.

"It was a beautiful, peaceful day with wonderful company. You were right about one thing. I needed the getaway even if it was only about 30 minutes from town. Thank you for forcing me out of the shop."

"That's all you're going to tell me?"

I smiled at her.

"Yes ma'am. That's all I'm going to tell you."

"You're horrible, Grace Ward. Do you know that? We worked so hard for you yesterday."

"Emmie, there's nothing to tell. Trevor and I are friends," I felt myself blushing as I said that. I wasn't a good liar, and after the kiss, I wondered if anything had changed. "We had a gorgeous picnic lunch, went out on the lake for a couple of hours. When I got back to his brother's lake house, he went into the kitchen to cook and shushed me out of there. I crashed on the couch. When I woke up, he'd prepared dinner."

"Uh huh. You know you're glowing this morning, don't you?"

I smiled, and Emmie sighed.

"A man who can cook – that's a dream of mine. And you're sure nothing happened after dinner, Grace?"

I stared at her and deliberately blinked several times without saying a word. She knew what that meant. It meant for her to back off.

"Is that Morse code? Are you trying to tell me something, Grace? I don't understand," she said as she folded her arms across her chest, trying to intimidate me.

"Friends, Emmie. Trevor and I are friends," I said emphasizing each word.

"If he didn't only have eyes for you, I swear I'd go after him since you only want him as a friend."

I glared back at her which caused her to burst into laughter.

"See, sweetie. I knew I'd get a rise out of you with that one. You want to be more than a friend to him, and you know it. I just don't know why you won't admit to it."

"Yes, I do. I love Trevor. But I have to get a few things taken care of before I can go any further into this relationship. I promise when anything changes, you'll be the third person to know. I admit it, but I want to be over Drew before I take my relationship with Trevor any further. And I'm not over him. I don't want to take too much baggage into another relationship. Speaking of Drew, he stopped by my apartment yesterday morning."

"Yes, we assumed as much when he came looking for you yesterday. And before I say this next part, remember I'm your best friend and I love you," she smiled and then took a deep breath. "You should probably go to a counselor with all the things you've gone through - if you don't want to take baggage into your relationship, that is."

I smiled at her and pulled the cards out of my purse. I flashed them at her.

"You're absolutely right. I have a couple of leads on those. I promise I'll call today to make an appointment. I need to check on Gemma this morning. I think she has a break around 10. I'm just going to show up and hope I catch her."

"Why do you need to check on her?"

"Are you still jealous, Emmie?"

"Sweetie, I was never jealous, but I don't know why you want to check on her so badly."

"Drew" -

"You're still helping him?" she narrowed her eyes at me as she asked.

"No, but Zack stopped by this morning and said he talked to

Drew yesterday. He thinks that Drew might be arresting her today. I know she didn't do it, and I have this feeling that if I go out there, I'll find something that will lead to the real killer."

"Whatever. I've got baby arrangements to make and a funeral pray."

"Good. I'll be back."

As I drove out to Augusta Tech, my mind wandered back to he story Drew told me of Dr. McKinney's presumed identity, and I wondered how it all fit together if it did at all. Drew wasn't sure, and he was the expert. I drove around the parking lot, looking for police vehicles or Drew's vehicle.

When I arrived, I stopped at Carolyn's office. I wanted to how her some photos I had of my mother's camellias. I couldn't find he ones I'd taken, but Mama had them on her phone and she texted hem to me. They were gorgeous. I didn't see Carolyn, however. Her loor was closed. I knocked, but there was no answer. I didn't try opening it. I headed to Gemma's office. Fortunately, she was there.

Her door was open, but I knocked anyway. She glanced up and gave me a broad smile.

"I didn't think you'd want to see me since everyone thinks I'm a murderer and won't talk to me anymore."

"I don't believe you're a murderer. I wish I could prove that to veryone."

She smiled and pointed to the chair in her office.

"Please have a seat. I don't have another class until 11. You came at the right time."

"I'm sorry I haven't called. I've been putting in long hours with the tournament coming up. There are a lot of parties I'm called on to help with."

"I understand. Is your husband any closer to finding the real iller?"

"He's my ex-husband, and I don't know all of the details of his nvestigation."

I wasn't a good liar, so I came up with a half-truth instead of the full truth. I knew some things about the investigation, but not everything.

"Where is Carolyn?"

"Oh, she's been talking for months about her trip to Greece. She leaves in a couple of days. She said she had some things to do before she went on the trip."

"I wanted to show her some pictures of " -

I didn't finish my sentence because as I sat in Gemma's office, I remembered the day of the murder and something Carolyn said about camellias reminding her of her hometown. She seemed to know a lot about them. I wondered why it hadn't occurred to me before. When that replayed in my brain, I could hear a twang in her voice I hadn't noticed before. She sounded a lot like Jazzy even though she tried to control her accent most of the time.

"What's the matter, Grace?"

"Gemma, did the police search Carolyn's office?"

"Why would they do that?"

"I don't know. Can we get in there?"

"We can try. What are you thinking?"

"I'm not sure, but I have a hunch."

I walked out of her office and down the hall to Carolyn's. I turned the knob, and to my surprise, the door opened. I walked in and surveyed the room. She'd removed everything personal. The desk had nothing on top of it except the phone and computer. There were no papers, no books, no pictures. It looked like she didn't plan to return from her trip to Greece.

"Where's all of her things?" asked Gemma.

"What was in here before?"

"She had photos, but it was odd. There were photos of places she'd been. It was like she didn't have any family. She never talked about any. She only had photos of places and knick-knacks from different travels. No photos of people."

"What are you looking for?"

"Anything; everything. I don't know."

"Anything? Can you be more specific, Grace?"

"Yes and no. I'll know it if I see it though. This is her office, isn't it?"

"Yes, I used to come in here a lot. I liked talking to her. Why is it empty? Grace, what are you thinking?"

I opened all the desk drawers; they were empty except for a few pens. Behind the desk was a bookshelf with cabinets on the bottom. I felt on top of each shelf, but I didn't find anything. I opened the cabinet doors. She seemed to leave nothing behind. I crawled under the desk and moved the chair. I opened her desk drawers a second time; surely, there was something.

I knelt down again and reached to the very back of the drawer, and this time, I felt something wedged between the drawer and the back of the desk. It was a desktop calendar and there was a business on it. It was for the Camellia City Bakery.

I just stared at it. Maybe this time, I really did crack a case, and maybe this time I couldn't blame anyone but myself if I ended up in danger.

"What is it, Grace?"

"Where does Carolyn live?"

"I have it written down in my office in my planner somewhere."

"You need to find it. I need it. It's so important."

She rushed back to her office, and I followed her. I needed to call Drew. And of all the times for him not to answer his phone.

"Drew, this is Grace. It's really important that I talk to you. Please call me as soon as you get this message."

Gemma flipped through the pages of her planner.

"Here it is," she said. "She lives on Kissingbower Road."

My brain started mapping out my route. Deans Bridge to Milledgeville to Kissingbower. I called Drew again. No answer so I sent him a text with Carolyn's address with the words "urgent" and "meet me there."

I tried not to speed. Of course, I got caught by every light at every intersection. At one point, I noticed by phone was ringing, but I couldn't pick it up because of Georgia's hands-free law. I'd have to wait until I could pull over. I didn't want to do that. It would waste time. If it was Drew who'd called, he would just have to meet me there.

The homes in that neighborhood were older. Carolyn's house was a quaint brick cottage with a front porch stoop and black awnings over the windows. Some of the homes had large, lush yards including Carolyn's, and I wasn't surprised to see the camellia bushes in the front yard. I wondered if there were more in the back. I was sure there were. I was sure they were beautiful too. Drew hadn't arrived when I'd gotten there. I glanced at my phone. It wasn't Drew who'd called; it was Emmie.

I sent Drew another text.

"Drew, please meet me at that address. NOW!"

I tried to gather my thoughts. I was going to show her my photographs, compliment her on her camellias, ask her if she knew the varieties, and I was going to record everything on my phone.

I knocked on the door. No one answered right away. I hoped I'd found the right house and wasn't knocking on some stranger's door. After I'd knocked a second time, Carolyn cracked open the door. She seemed surprised as she opened the door.

"Grace, how are you doing?"

"I stopped to see Gemma today, but I wanted to show you my mother's camellia bushes. We'd talked about propagating them."

"Oh yes, of course, I'm surprised you remembered."

"Carolyn, I never forget a flower lover."

She started to drop her guard, but she acted nervous.

"Would you like to come around back?"

"Sure."

She walked through the front door without letting me see inside. I followed her around to the back of the house, and she opened the ivy-covered gate allowing me to enter her beautiful gardens. The back yard was smaller than I thought. There were sever

154

towering pines.

"When I bought this house, I wanted camellias. It was perfect, and you can never have too many. Can you?" she queried. She still had a nervous edge in her voice, and a bit of a Cajun twang similar to Jazzy's came through.

"No, you can't."

I tried to remember my script. I had a list of questions. I was afraid to pull out the photos now. I'd frantically called Drew and texted him. I didn't need him responding in the middle of my showing her the photographs.

"What varieties do you have?"

"I called an extension agent from the University of Georgia to come out and look at them," she said. "But he told me there were more than 3,000 varieties."

"Yes, that's true. Did you know that the camellia is Alabama's state flower?"

I was going to have to stall. I needed Drew to get here. I hoped he'd gotten my messages.

"He told me that. I do have some beautiful pink ones. They are not too pale and not too bright. There's another bush with gorgeous red ones."

"My mother has similar colors. I do have some photos of them. Where would you like to put some?"

"I have the perfect spot," she said and walked to an open spot by a fence.

As she did, I sent another text to Drew.

"We're in the back yard. Please hurry."

Almost immediately after sending it, I thought I heard what sounded like a text alert. My heart started racing. Was I imagining that or just hoping it could've been him?

"A white one or another shade of pink would be best here," she said.

"When you get back from Greece, we should get together. I have the perfect one from my mother's yard."

She smiled at me, but it was an odd smile – a smile that seemed to say the wearer knew something no one else did.

"Does this remind you of home, Carolyn? Does it remind you of growing up in Slidell, Louisiana?"

Her smile disappeared as she raised an eyebrow at me.

"I don't believe I ever told anyone where I grew up."

"You grew up with your younger brother, Thomas McKinley, who died about 30 years ago when he was in college."

Her face turned ashen as she narrowed her eyes at me. She shook her head in disbelief.

"And you knew his college friend, James Mitchell?"

"No, I don't know what you're talking about," she sputtered, but her expression had given everything away.

"The same James Mitchell who stole your brother's identity but altered it slightly," I continued.

"How do you know this? No one knew this."

Tears began to form in her eyes. She stopped looking at me and glanced past me. I heard the gate close. She started shaking her head. I glanced over my shoulder to see Drew walking.

"I didn't tell anyone."

"I know," I said.

"I'd been looking for him for 30 years. But I'd been looking under the wrong name. I didn't know he stole my brother's name and birth certificate. I lived in Virginia not too far from where that play was held – the play he stole from Ms. Johnston, and I saw the article I saw his picture. He looked a lot like my daddy at that age. I couldn't believe it," she said as tears poured down her face. "Gemma whined so much about that stupid play – how she couldn't believe he'd do something like that to her. That was nothing compared to what he did to me, what he did to my family."

She paused.

"It doesn't matter now. I have nothing. He took it all away from me. My brother, Thomas, was a football star in high school. He wanted to be an engineer. He had a full ride at school. I waited until the perfect moment to confront him. I learned a thing or two about getting the security cameras offline so no one would see anything. I made him think that Ms. Johnston wanted to see him in the theater. She needed his help. I knew it would appeal to his ego."

She paused and glanced to the ground. Her shoulders shook as she cried. She looked up at me. She didn't talk to Drew although he was listening to everything she had to say.

"He didn't know who I was even though I'd met him that summer he'd spent at our house and that Thanksgiving. It was scary how much he and Thomas looked alike. When I confronted him, Dr. McKinney said it was an accident, but why steal his money? Why leave his body in a burned-out car? Why did he take my baby brother's name and change it ever so slightly? He didn't answer any of it. He didn't care. He was arrogant until the very end. I was furious. As he started to walk away, I grabbed the nearest thing I could find and just hit him. And I couldn't stop hitting him. I stood there and felt nothing. I changed in the dressing room and took my clothes with me. No one ever noticed me here anyway. They didn't notice me when I left either."

She paused again. There was a fire in her eyes as she continued.

"I don't regret it. After Thomas died, my father started drinking. He was killed in a car accident two years after Thomas died. My mother's heart couldn't take it. She died of a broken heart a year to the day after Daddy died. James Mitchell took everything from me; everyone I held dear. I'm all alone now. Arrest me. I don't care. I have nothing to live for anymore."

Drew walked back to the gate and let in two uniformed deputies who put handcuffs on her and read her rights to her.

My heart dropped as I watched. I could feel the tears streaming down my own cheeks. Yes, what she'd done was horrible, but I'd felt her pain in my dream. I felt it now as I watched her. The pain was of a woman who'd gotten revenge but not for herself. The sorrow that weighed her down represented a lifetime of loss.

I stood in her garden as the deputies took her away. I wiped my tears. I was almost afraid to turn and look at Drew. My hands were trembling. I think my whole body was.

"What were you thinking, Grace?"

I knew Drew's angry voice well, and surprisingly, that's not the voice I heard. It was tender; it was concerned. I could tell he wasn't happy, but he wasn't mad either. I wasn't sure what to make of it. I swallowed hard as I glanced at him.

"I was thinking that a prime murder suspect was about to leave the country if I didn't do something, and I tried calling you and texting you several times. I brought you to the right place."

He walked toward me and reached out to take my hand.

"You don't take matters into your own hands. You never go alone. What if she'd had a gun?"

"She didn't."

"But you had no way of knowing that, Grace. What if I hadn't gotten here in time?"

I didn't say anything. Part of me wanted him to hold me, and it hurt that I couldn't throw myself into his arms. I'd spent the past few weeks wanting to avoid him, but now, I didn't want to leave him.

"I knew you would."

I choked out the words because the emotions were starting to overwhelm me.

"Hunch?"

"No, Drew, I know you."

He seemed surprised when I said that. He let go of my hand.

"Grace, if anything ever happened to you, I'd never forgive myself."

"I know. That's the reason I was sure you'd be here."

He took a deep breath and let go of my hand.

"How did you know it was her?"

I shrugged my shoulders.

"It all goes back to what I do best – flowers." I said and then smiled. "It all had to do with a conversation about camellias and the way she talked at times reminded me of Jazzy. Her accent was faint as though she tried to hide it. I knew Slidell, Louisiana is nicknamed the 'Camellia City.' I know lots of useless flower facts except that this time, they weren't useless. It took me a little time to remember that she said flowers reminded her of her hometown. You'd said that Thomas McKinley lived near New Orleans. Slidell is about 45 minutes away. I had a dream last night that Jazzy told me I knew the answer. When I went to see Gemma today, it jarred that memory loose. We searched Carolyn's office. It was empty except for a calendar, which is in my car. It was from Slidell. My hunch paid off."

He put his hands on his hips and smiled.

"Good job, Grace. I owe you on this one."

"You're welcome, Drew. By the way, she wouldn't let me in the house, so there's something in there she didn't want me to see. Can I go in with you?"

He raised an eyebrow as he turned toward the gate and walked back to the house. I followed him. The door was partially opened.

"Don't touch anything," he said.

The hardwood floors creaked as we walked into the tiny living room at the front of the house. There was no furniture in the room just a few boxes. The tiny kitchen had a small table with one chair. The house had two bedrooms. One had a bed and a dresser on which were multiple framed photographs. I recognized Thomas McKinley immediately. He looked like a younger version of Dr. McKinney. There also was a photograph of two infants, and another of the family of five. They looked happy in the picture.

I followed Drew into the second bedroom. The walls were covered with newspaper articles about her missing brother and his death. There was an article about her father's drunk driving accident and death. He'd been a respected physician, and the reactions were sadness at his death. And then there were articles about James Mitchell aka J.C. McKinney. I knew there had to be more to this man than I'd found. She had original newspaper clippings plus there were some that appeared to be printouts from the years before she discovered his new identity. I also saw the article I'd found about the play and the photograph of him.

I stood and stared at the findings.

"I feel so bad for her. All of this is so sad, Drew. She's spent her life trying to get revenge. How sad. What a waste."

"Murder investigations always are sad and hard," said Drew. " think part of me dies every time I do one."

I turned to look at him when he said that. Had I ever though about how he felt about the investigations? In so many ways, he seemed to be in control of those emotions. It was the murder-suicide closest to him that sent him over the edge. But what had seeing death on a regular basis done to him? He saw it even before he was a homicide investigator. He saw the horrible side of human beings. Pa of me still wanted to comfort him, help him. A year ago, my respons would've been completely different. I lightly touched his arm.

"I think I understand that, Drew."

He smiled. He covered my hand with his and stared at it for a moment before letting go. I followed his lead and moved my hand. He glanced back at me, and I could see the pain in his eyes. I needed to go, but there was a sense of finality with me leaving. I wasn't sure why I still hadn't accepted everything that had happened. Nothing had changed. Nothing was going to change. I'm not sure why I'd hoped that it would. I needed to get over him.

"I guess I should leave to let you collect your evidence. Gemma will be happy at least. Maybe she can do her gala after all. I wonder why Carolyn tried to pin it on her?"

"If I find out, I'll let you know."

"Thanks."

There was another awkward pause.

"Drew, does therapy really help?"

He seemed surprised at the question, but he gave me a soft smile before answering.   "Yeah, it really does especially when you combine it with other things. Are you going to see someone?"

"I promised Trevor I would."

"I'm glad. It will help you move on," he glanced away as he said that.

"I need to get going. Goodbye, Drew."

"Goodbye, Grace, and thank you for your help once again."

I walked out the front door and got into my car. I didn't want to cry anymore. The tears didn't seem to care what I wanted though; they coursed down my cheeks with abandon. I felt lost. Trevor was working at the clinic, and I didn't want to go home. I got in my car and started driving. I knew my shop was in good hands. If I didn't return immediately, I wouldn't go out of business.

I drove to the Savannah River and found my spot near the park, where I could look out and see the beautiful houses across the way in North Augusta. In my heart, I knew there was nothing left of my relationship with Drew, so I sat there resolving to take control of my life and all areas of it. I reached into my purse and pulled out the card. Theresa Wyatt was the name on the card. I called and got an appointment for the week after Masters. I felt a sense of relief. Maybe there was a way to heal.

I finally made it back to the shop, where Emmie greeted me with a huge hug.

"What are you doing, Emmie? I can't breathe."

"Congrats on solving the murder."

I stared at her as she let me go.

"How did you know?"

"Well, there was something on the radio about an arrest. You weren't mentioned per se, but the sheriff thanked the community for their tips."

I laughed.

"It was something else."

I gave her the condensed version.

"Why are you here, Grace? I have everything under control; Jazzy was coming to take over and close."

"I know, but I didn't want to go home, and Trevor is still at the clinic."

"You need a break."

"I'm okay, Emmie. You don't have to stay here. Oh, and I made some decisions."

Emmie tilted her head.

"What kind?"

"I'm going to counseling. I set up an appointment for the second week in April, and remember when I said, you'd be the third to know something? Well, you're the second to know it."

I wasn't sure the exact word for her response. I guess "squeal" would probably describe the noise that came out of her mouth. As she jumped up and down and hugged me while still jumping up and down, making me jump with her.

"That is the best news I've heard in months, sweetie. I'm so happy for you."

"Well, how about keep it quiet until I talk to Trevor. Okay?"

"I'll try really hard, but I'm not making any promises. What color will your bridesmaid's wear? Remember, I don't look good in pink."

I laughed.

"Seriously? Let's take it once step at a time."

"You won't do a Christmas wedding again, and you are so not a fall person. July and August are too hot plus your birthday is in July. June is overdone. May is good."

"That's only two months away."

"And why do you need forever to decide?"

"Stop. We aren't even dating yet. And he'll have to ask me to marry him. It may be the 21st century, but he'll have to do the asking at least on that part."

"Fine. I've got to pick up the boys. I'm glad you made it back. Jazzy will be here shortly, but I'm going to leave since you're here."

She hugged me again so tightly that I could barely breathe.

"I'm so excited for you, sweetie. I need to do some sketches. I have ideas."

"Go, Emmie. Just go."

She squealed again as she rushed out the back door.

I went into my office and sat at the computer. I was deep in thought until I heard the bell ring. I glanced up, and it was after 6. I'd forgotten to lock up.

I walked out into the shop to see Trevor leaning on the counter.

"Good evening, sir. May I help you?" I asked in my most professional tone.

He stood up and winked at me.

"I was hoping that you might be able to make a floral arrangement. I know it's late, and you're getting ready to close. There's a beautiful woman I'd like to ask to dinner tonight, and she loves fresh flowers."

"Did you have anything specific in mind?"

"I know she loves delphinium elatum; I'm told that's the proper name for larkspur, and her favorites are blue."

"I'm sorry, sir. I would have to special order it. It's not in season. It's a summer flower."

"That makes sense because it's the flower of July; the month she was born."

I laughed.

"I'm still trying to figure out where you got them in December, Trevor. I know what it takes to get flowers from specialty greenhouses at Christmas."

He winked again.

"I have my sources."

"So, are you asking me to dinner?"

"Yes, Grace Ward, I'm asking you to have dinner with me. I believe we have something to celebrate."

"We do?"

I wasn't sure what he was talking about. He pushed his phone toward me. He had a screenshot from the newspaper's website of the article about Carolyn's arrest.

"I see your rabbit trail paid off. I'm sure you had something to do with this. You must've realized who did it."

"I did, and that's not the only thing I realized today, Trevor."

He raised an eyebrow.

"Really?"

"I realized that I needed to make an appointment with that therapist you suggested, and I have one set up for after Masters."

"That's a great start, Grace."

I took a breath before saying what was on my mind.

"Last night, when you kissed me" -

I glanced up to see him smiling at me.

"I should apologize for that," he said. "That wasn't a 'just friends' type of kiss."

"No, it wasn't. But don't apologize. Last night when you kissed me, I realized I hadn't felt that way during a kiss in a long time. I've been dead inside. I died with each miscarriage; I died with each fight with Drew; I died with each drink he took. I died as my marriage died. I died with each murder case. I was running on autopilot; just existing, functioning. What wasn't dead hurt so much. I saw no need to save me – as you said. I mean why go to a counselor when you're dead or dying? What does it matter?"

He didn't say anything.

"But when you kissed me, I realized I wasn't dead, after all. Something inside me was very much alive."

He smiled at me.

"I haven't felt alive in so long, Trevor. So, I'm asking you if you'd like to go on a date with me."

He walked around to my side of the counter and put his hands around my waist, pulling me close to him.

"Grace, I'd love to go out on a date with you. I'm glad you are starting to feel alive again," he said. "But I can't date you right now, Grace."

I felt my heart plummet into my stomach.

"It's not what you think," he said as he gently caressed my

cheek. "You're starting to feel, and I know there's a lot of pain in there still. As you go through this and go through the pain of healing, I don't want you to think you're a burden to me. That's not true. Before I go on a date with you as something other than a friend, I want you to feel whole. Talking with a therapist is going in the right direction. I'm not going anywhere. I promise. I will be with you every step of the way."

"Can I ask you a favor, Trevor?"

"Of course."

"I want to restore your mother's gardens. Flowers, gardening, soil – all of that has healing properties. And I remember she had such beautiful gardens. They could be beautiful again. I could make them beautiful again."

He smiled.

"If she was still here, I think she'd love that idea. I know she hated seeing them fall into ruin. Hiring someone to do the work wasn't the same to her."

"I've sketched out some of my plans. And I really miss being around camellias, azaleas, roses and all of the beautiful flowers and shrubs she had."

"Whatever you want, Grace. We'll make it happen. You take care of healing, and that will give me some time to plan an amazing and memorable first date."

"Dr. Blake, I still remember our first date all those years ago in high school. It was my very first date with anyone, and we went to the homecoming game where Dana Andrews was crowned homecoming queen. Our team won, and then we went to the dance. I had a gorgeous blue dress. You were so handsome in your suit. You asked me out the following night, and we went out for pizza and miniature golf."

He smiled.

"Yes, and you beat me."

"See, our first dates were memorable."

"Okay, then. How about a memorable second first date? I

have better ideas and a larger budget."

I laughed.

"Any time spent with you is memorable. We could eat a sandwich off a food truck at the Augusta Common, and it would be memorable as long as I was with you. You don't have to spend a lot of money. But you do have a deal. I'll go to therapy and work in your mother's garden, and I'll focus on healing. Because I do want to have that second first date with you."

He smiled and kissed my forehead.

"How about some Mexican food tonight?" I asked.

"If that's how you want to celebrate solving a murder, I'm in," he said.

MURDER TAKES A BOW

If you liked the book, please leave a review.

If you like mysteries, please read my Victoria James' mystery series. The first in the series is Murder at Twin Oaks. https://www.amazon.com/dp/B00MUC5JE8

CPSIA information can be obtained
at www.ICGtesting.com
Printed in the USA
LVHW041110111119
636959LV00006B/2366